LAW OF THE ROPE
THE CROCKETTS' WESTERN SAGA: 3

ROBERT VAUGHAN

WOLFPACK
PUBLISHING
— EST 2013 —

Published in the United States by Wolfpack Publishing, Las Vegas

Wolfpack Publishing
5130 S. Fort Apache Road, 215-380
Las Vegas, NV 89148

wolfpackpublishing.com

Paperback ISBN 978-1-64734-635-5
eBook ISBN 978-1-64734-634-8

LAW OF THE ROPE

Chapter One

Clay County, Missouri

"You could come with Frank and me," Jesse James said. "We're startin' our own gang."

Will Crockett shook his head. "I appreciate the offer, Jesse, but for me, the war is over."

"Don't get me wrong, Will, what we're doing has nothing to do with the war. We're not claiming to be fightin' for the South the way we were when you and I rode for Quantrill. No sir, we're doing it for ourselves." Jesse laughed. "And believe me it beats plowin' behind a team of mules. It'll pay better too."

"Maybe if I was going to stay in Missouri, I would take you up on your offer. But my brother didn't come back with me, and I promised to meet him in New Mexico."

"How is old Gid?" Jesse asked.

"Well fed and happy," Will replied with a smile

"That's the way I remember him," Jesse said.

"Jesse! Jesse! There's a posse a comin'!" a man shouted as he ran toward Jesse.

"Damnit, we talked to the sheriff; he promised there'd be no trouble if we didn't do anything here in Jackson County."

"It don't look like Sheriff Pemberton's with 'em. Don't see nobody I recognize, neither."

"Get mounted, boys, we're gettin' outta here," Jesse called, running toward his own horse.

Will had no choice but to get mounted with the rest of them, and then gallop away.

Shots were exchanged in the galloping getaway, but not one of Jesse's men was hit. The pursuers weren't as lucky. Will saw at least two go down, though as he was not firing, he knew he was not responsible for either one of them.

It soon became evident that nobody in the posse was from Jackson County as Jesse and his gang were able to evade them by following streams and hidden trails. Less than half an hour after the chase had started, it was over.

"Didn't I tell you boys ole' Jesse would get us out of that?" one of the men said. "Hell, we got away as slick as a whistle."

"I noticed you weren't shooting," Jesse said as he rode up to Will.

"I didn't figure it was my fight," Will said. "They were

after you, they weren't after me."

"You ran away with us."

"I don't think I had much of a choice, because I wasn't sure they knew they weren't after me."

Jesse laughed. "You're right about that." Jesse stroked his chin for a moment. "You're a good man, Will, and I wish you and your brother would join us, but I'm not going to insist. I figure you're going to do whatever you have to do. But if you ever change your mind, you'll always be welcome."

"I appreciate that, Jesse, and I wish all of you the best of luck."

With a tip of his hat Will left Jesse, Frank, and the others, and started riding south. Ten days after leaving the James Gang, Will reached his home town of St. Leger, in Ozark County, Missouri. Going into the Nippy Jones Saloon, he was greeted by the owner.

"Will Crockett," Nippy said. "I haven't seen you in a month of Sundays. Where you been keeping yourself?"

"Oh, here and there," Will answered. "Texas, mostly."

"Where's your brother? Is Gid with you?"

"Gid said there wasn't anything here for him anymore, so he didn't come with me. And I guess he's right. This was home for a long time, and I thought I'd pay this place one more visit."

"I can see why you might want to come back for a bit,"

Nippy said. He drew a beer, then set the mug in front of Will. "but iffen I was you, I'd keep your time here short."

"Why is that?"

"They's paper out on you 'n your brother with a five-hundred-dollar reward, dead or alive."

"Why?"

"Actually they's paper out on ever'one of you'ns that ever rode for Quantrill or Anderson," Nippy said. "Jesse 'n Frank James has got the most money offered for them, but you 'n Gid is next.

"The Yankees up at Jefferson City say they's ashamed of anyone that rode with Quantrill, 'n they ain't to be treated as regular soldiers. The sheriff plans to put all of 'em in jail, 'n you 'n Gid in particular 'cause you kilt Otto Hoffman."

"Damn, Sheriff Goff knows that Hoffman murdered my parents. Why would he do that?"

Nippy shook his head. "Goff ain't the sheriff no more. The new sheriff is a fella by the name of Atkinson, 'n he wasn't elected. He was appointed by the Yankee governor we got."

"Well, I don't plan on staying very long. I'm going to stop by the cemetery to pay my respects to ma and pa's graves, then I thought I'd ride out to take a look at what used to be our farm."

"Nippy nodded his head. "Well, it was good seein' you

again, 'n maybe when this all blows over, you 'n your brother can come back home. In the meantime, tell Gid we miss him."

"I'll do that."

Toby Johnson was sitting at a table close enough to overhear the conversation between Nippy and Will. Like the rest of Missouri, Ozark County had been divided in its loyalties during the war, and Johnson had been one of those who had fought with the North. Will Crockett had said that he was going to ride out to the farm his family had once owned. Johnson knew where that farm was, and he also knew about the reward that was being offered for the Crocketts. It said dead or alive.

As unobtrusively as possible, Johnson left the saloon. He had heard Crockett say he was going to the cemetery first, so he knew that would give him time to get out to the farm, and get in position to set up an ambush. He rubbed his hands together. Five hundred dollars would soon be his.

There were no structures left on the farm. They had all been burned down on the day a group of Jayhawkers led by Otto Hoffman had raided the farm and killed Drury and Amanda Crockett. In fact, Toby Johnson had led Hoffman to the farm. Most of the people who lived in Ozark County knew that Johnson had fought for the

North, but very few knew that early in the war, he had ridden with Hoffman.

Johnson left the Jayhawkers not long after the Crockett raid, to join the Missouri 21st Mounted Infantry. That had saved his life, because few remembered that Toby had once been a part of the Kansas Redlegs. Will and Gid Crockett had hunted down and killed every surviving Jayhawker who had taken part in the murder of their parents. They did not kill Johnson for the simple reason that they didn't know he had been a part of Hoffman's group.

Tying his horse off at the foot of a hill that would shield him from view of anyone approaching, Johnson snaked his rifle from the saddle sheath, then climbed to the top of the hill and lay down just behind the crest. He jacked a round into the chamber and waited.

Will approached Possum Walk Creek, then stopped long enough to look down at the sun-dancing highlights on the water. He smiled as a memory came back to him.

"I'll bet this is the biggest catfish that has ever been caught in the whole world!" eight-year-old Gideon Crockett said as he held the still-flopping fish up to show it off to his pa and his brother.

"Nah-uh, that's not the biggest in the whole world," Will replied.

"You don't know."

"Yes I do know 'cause I'm older 'n you," Will replied.

Urging his horse on across the stream he continued up the road that was once known as Crockett Lane. At this point he could almost believe that the house where he had been born was still there because it wouldn't be in view yet. Not until he crossed the hill in front of him, would he be able to see exactly where the house had been.

He stopped before going over the hill. For just a moment, he could almost convince himself that when he crested the hill he would see the house and barn. His pa would be sharpening a plow, and his ma would be cooking supper.

"All right, let's go," he said as he leaned forward to pat his horse on the neck. His leaning forward was a fortuitous act because at that precise moment, he heard the crack of a bullet passing over his head.

Looking up quickly, he saw a little puff of white smoke showing him where the shooter was. He could tell by the sound that the shooter was using a rifle, and that meant he would have to take the time to jack another round into the chamber. Will used that time not to run away, but to charge up the hill, taking the chance the shooter would rush his second shot, and that is exactly what happened.

The second shot missed him by a wider margin than

had the first, and before the shooter could ready his rifle for a third attempt, Will had reached the top of the hill. He had his pistol out and looking to his left saw the shooter, now fully exposed.

"Drop that rifle!" Will shouted.

Instead of complying with the order, the shooter whirled around to point his rifle but before he could get off another shot, Will pulled the trigger and saw the shooter grab his chest then fall back. Dismounting, Will hurried over to him, keeping his gun ready.

"I'll be damn," he said quietly when he recognized the man who had been shooting at him. "Toby Johnson."

Johnson was dead, and for a moment or two, Will wondered what to do with the body. Enough people had seen Will since he had come back that if Johnson was discovered here at the old Crockett farm, Will might well become a suspect.

Looking around, Will found Johnson's horse so he tied the body belly down on the saddle, gave the horse a slap on the rump, and sent it away. The horse would return to someplace familiar to it and there would be no reason to connect Johnson with Will.

If there was a reward out on him that even Toby Johnson was willing to try and collect, Will knew that his best bet was to get out of Missouri immediately.

He wished he had gone to New Mexico with Gid.

Chapter Two

Gideon Crockett stood half a head taller than most men, and had shoulders as broad as an axe handle.

"He ain't the kind of feller that you'd want to get crosswise with," someone once said of him, and the observation had not been disputed.

At the moment Gid was squatting down in a dry creek channel that ran through the Mimbre Mountain Range in New Mexico. A moment earlier he had seen a flash of color and he had dismounted so he could get a closer look.

The color that he had seen did not seem to be a part of an embedded vein of gold. Instead there appeared to be quite a few pieces of rock just scattered across the surface, or barely imbedded. Gid picked up one of the rocks, then whistled quietly.

"Well now, what have we here?" he asked.

After a moment of observation, he knew exactly what it was.

"Damn, it's gold!"

Gid brushed away some of the dirt and found, on the bed of the dry creek, at least two dozen more nuggets that were as big or bigger than the first one. With a triumphant smile he began gathering them up.

Where did they come from? Gid knew that people often panned for gold but if there was no water, it only made sense that any gold would settle to the bottom.

Gid took his saddle bags from his horse and quickly consolidated them. He filled the empty bag with the gathered nuggets, then had a look around, trying to ascertain where the gold had come from.

The dry creek bed was flanked by a steep ridge and Gid decided to climb it to see if he could find color somewhere that might suggest a vein.

The first part of the climb was easy enough, but the second part was through the treeless, beige colored terrain which was loose rock and shale. From here, climbing became more difficult and Gid discovered that the best way was to be on all fours, hand over foot. Scaling the ridge near the low point of the saddle, he found that the ridge was only a foot or so wide, which made it difficult to safely traverse the ridge line for more than several feet in either direction. The only way he could do so was to straddle the ridge.

The drop off on the far side was steep enough to discourage any thought of climbing down into the adjoining canyon, and for a moment Gid stopped to consider how dumb he was to have put himself into such a position. He could quite easily fall which would be disastrous because he was out here all alone.

"You were right, Will, I don't have any business climbing around out here all by myself. Damnit, I hate it when you're always right." Even though he was alone, he spoke the words aloud just to hear a human voice, even if it was his own.

Slowly, and very carefully, Gid climbed back down until once more, he was safely in the dry creek.

Gid took out a pencil and a piece of paper from the saddle bag that held his personal items. He wrote on the paper.

This area, to include all mineral rights: heron and adjacent to, is under claim by

Gideon and William Crockett

Signed, Gideon Crockett

Gid had eaten a can of peaches for his lunch and he put the paper in the can, then gathering some stones, made a cairn around it. He knew this would establish legal claim to the site until he could file a proper claim on it in the county court.

Before coming on his prospecting adventure Gid had drawn out a calendar so he could keep track of the days. Checking it out, he saw that it was about time for him to get back to Thornburg, where he and Will had planned to meet.

"Big brother, have I got a surprise for you," he said as he mounted his horse for the ride to the town. "I hope you're back from Missouri."

The shock waves of the explosion moved across the field and hit Will Crockett, making his stomach shake. The blasts were set off by long fuses, but were timed to go together, starting as bursts of white-hot flame causing black smoke to erupt from under the points where the charges were laid. The underpinnings of the trestle were carried away by the torpedoes, but the superstructure remained intact for several more seconds, stretching across the creek with no visible means of support, as if defying the laws of gravity. Then, slowly, the tracks began to sag and the ties started snapping, popping with a series of loud reports like pistol shots, until finally, with a resounding crash and a splash of water, the whole bridge collapsed into the creek.

"Now, that's the way to do it, boys," Quantrill said exultantly. "We dropped her into the water just as neat as a pin!"

"The Yankees won't be movin' troops over this railroad for a while," Gid Crockett said.

"I suppose not," Will replied.

"What's wrong, Big Brother?" Gid asked. "You don't sound very pleased about it. It was a good job, and it'll deny the Yankees the use of this road."

"Gid, don't you remember when they built this trestle? We watched them build it, and we were glad because it would cut two hours off a trip to Kansas City. Do you remember how long it took them to build it?"

"No."

"It took six weeks," Will said. "Six weeks to build, and we just destroyed it in six seconds. We did it to stop the Yankees, but it was our bridge in the first place. The tracks, the bridges, the roads, all these things we are destroying belong to the people of Missouri...to us. What kind of war is it when we strike at the enemy by destroying the property of our own people?"

"It's a terrible war, Will, but that's the kind of war we've got," Gid said. "And it's better to destroy one of our own bridges than to give the Yankees one of our towns."

"I understand that," Will said. "But, just because I understand something, doesn't mean I have to agree with it."

"Thornburg," Gid said.

"What?"

"Thornburg."

"What are you talking about?"

"Thornburg!" the conductor called, coming through the car.

Will, who had been sleeping, opened his eyes.

"Thornburg!" the conductor shouted again. "Next stop is Thornburg, New Mexico. Anybody gettin' off in Thornburg, this is your stop!"

Will laughed. So, that was how Thornburg worked its way into his dream.

He stretched, trying to get the kinks and soreness out. He had been riding a train for three days now, having boarded back in Kansas City, Missouri. It was the first time, since the war, that he had visited Missouri. And he had made the trip alone, his brother Gid opting not to go with him.

"A bad dream?" The voice was soft and melodic, a woman's voice.

"Beg your pardon?" Will replied.

"You were scowling as you awoke," the woman said. The woman was petite, with green eyes and red curls framing an oval face. Her nose was straight and thin, and her mouth rather full, with ruby lips that were wet and slightly puckered. She was wearing a watch, pinned to her dress as if it were a broach.

"I suppose it was," Will said, not willing to share the

real dream with anyone. "But, I've already forgotten it."

"Dreams are sometimes fleeting," the woman said. Smiling, she extended her hand. "My name is Lurleen Simpson."

"I'm Will Crockett. I see you have a watch, Miss Simpson. Can you tell me the time?"

"It's 11:30," Lurleen said. "This watch was a gift from my uncle when I came west and it keeps perfect time. I call it my schoolmarm watch. Will you be getting off at Thornburg, Will Crockett?"

"Yes."

"How long will you be staying?"

"I don't know," Will replied. "I'm supposed to meet my brother here, so I guess it all depends on when he shows up."

"I hope he doesn't show up too soon."

"Why is that?"

Lurleen smiled. "Let's just say I am a woman of opportunity. If you have to wait around for a few days, perhaps you will come visit me at The Desert Strike Saloon."

"The Desert Strike Saloon? Isn't it a little unusual for a schoolmarm to spend time in a saloon?"

Lurleen smiled, but she didn't answer Will's question. Instead, she pulled something from her handbag and handed it to him. "Be sure to bring this with you, when you come," she said.

When Will examined the brass coin she handed him, he knew immediately what it was. Called a chit, it was stamped, Good for one visit. Such chits were used by prostitutes as a means of payment for their services. The chits were then redeemable for money at the bar. In some towns Will knew the chits were treated as legal tender and could be exchanged for face value at the local bank.

Lurleen was a whore! He would never have guessed that, and he looked at her in surprise.

Lurleen chuckled at the expression on his face. "I know, I don't look like a soiled dove, do I?" She asked. "At least, I certainly hope I don't, not now, anyway, that's because I'm just returning from a visit with my aunt and uncle back in Memphis. They think I'm teaching school out here."

"So, that's what you meant by the schoolmarm watch?"

Lurleen nodded. "Actually, there is some truth to it. I did start out as a schoolteacher," she explained. "But when the school superintendent's daughter decided she wanted the job, I was fired."

"I'm sorry."

Lurleen smiled, prettily. "Don't be sorry. I'm making a lot more money now and, believe me, I'm having a hell of a lot more fun!"

"You can't make money by giving these things away," Will said, holding up the chit.

"Honey, I don't give them to everyone," she said. "But I was watching you while you were sleeping. You can tell a lot about a man by watching him when he sleeps. I think you would be the kind of customer I like to have. Your first time with me will be free. But all other times...and I'm counting on there being other times...you will have to pay for the privilege. Call this an advertisement."

"All right," Will said. "I'll take you up on your offer. This may be just the thing to get rid of three days of train weariness."

"For you and me both, honey," Lurleen said throatily.

The train slowed, brakes squealing, then jerked to a stop. Only three people from the car got up to leave: Will, Lurleen, and a drummer. The drummer, with cases in both hands, blocked the exit way for a moment, but neither Lurleen nor Will hurried him. The remaining passengers stayed in their seats, their minds and bodies too travel-weary to pay any attention to the exodus.

Will's first priority, after seeing to his baggage, was to go down to the livery stable to check on his horse. He had left the animal there six weeks earlier when he took the train to Missouri.

"Yes, sir, Mr. Crockett, your horse is doin' fine," the stableman said. "I've fed him every day, let him out for exercise, and rubbed him down."

"Thanks, Jasper," Will said. "I appreciate it."

"You were a good customer, payin' in advance like you done," Jasper said. "Your saddle and tack are here, too. Will you be leaving now?"

"Not yet," Will said. "I'm going to meet my brother here, so I'm afraid you'll have to put my horse up for a few more days. Do you have the space for him?"

"Sure do, Mr. Crockett. Be glad to have your horse for as long as you want him to stay."

Chapter Three

When Will checked in at the Saint Albans hotel, he unpacked, then took a bottle of whiskey from his grip and poured himself a generous water-glass full. He drank it without water, except for the last swallow, which he used to brush his teeth.

After he was settled in his room, Will went next door to The Desert Strike Saloon. Lurleen was just coming down the stairs when Will arrived and the transformation in the young woman was amazing.

She had been pretty on the train—mousey—but pretty. Then, she had exhibited the innocence of that breed of woman that Will often saw but never touched. She looked as if she belonged to what Will referred to as, "the other life." The other life consisted of hard-working, honest men who ranched or farmed, who drove wagons or stagecoaches, who clerked in stores and worked in offices. It also consisted of the women and children who were there in support of those same hard-working, honest men.

Though Will referred to them as the other life, it wasn't a derisive sobriquet. On the contrary, they were people he admired, respected, and envied. Will and his brother lived in a world that was parallel to, but not a part of, the other life. Had there not been a war, had things not been so drastically changed by events over which he had no control...he might have been one of those people, and a woman, such as the woman he had mistaken Lurleen for, might be his.

The world in which Will and his brother now lived was one of transience and a surprising amount of violence. And the women in this life were like the woman who was now standing at the bottom of the stairs smiling seductively at him. There was very little resemblance between this woman and the woman he had met on the train.

Will walked over to her.

"I believe this is yours," he said handing her the brass chit.

Lurleen had a broad smile, as she extended her hand to Will.

Gid Crockett rode into Gold Hill, New Mexico, leading a pack-mule. He was a big man, who right now was wearing a bushy beard and uncustomary long hair. Almost two months before, Gid had said goodbye to his brother at the depot in Thornburg, New Mexico. Not since then had he seen civilization, having spent the time in the mountains prospecting for gold.

The adventure had produced some results, though how successful he had been, he didn't yet know. He was bringing back two saddlebags full of color-showing ore. Just how well he had done would depend upon the assayer's report.

Gold Hill was a mining town with both gold and silver being dug from the hills. Because of that, Gid's arrival, complete with pack mule and prospecting equipment, elicited absolutely no curiosity from any of the citizens. It was a typical western town, fly-blown, with a single street, lined on both sides by unpainted, rip-sawn, false-fronted buildings. It could have been any of several hundred towns in a dozen western states.

As he rode by, a couple of half-naked whores, their breasts spilling over the top of the chemises they were wearing, stood on a balcony and called down to him.

"Hey, darlin'!" one of them greeted.

"Just get into town?" the other asked.

Gid smiled, nodded, and touched the brim of his hat by way of returning their greeting.

"Come on up and keep us company. We'll give you a good welcome," one of the whores said.

"Miss, until I get a bath, I'm not even fit company for my horse," Gid said as he rode under her.

The other whore pinched her nose and, exaggerating, made a waving motion with her hand. "Oh, honey, you've got that right," she teased.

Laughing, Gid rode on down the street until he reached a small building at the far end. A sign in front of the building read, "Milton Bell, Assayer."

Gid looked up at the sign, then swung down from his saddle and tied his horse and mule off at the hitching rail. Hefting the saddlebags over one shoulder, he stepped inside. A bell, hanging on the front door dinged as he walked in.

"Be right with you," a disembodied voice called from the back of the building. A moment later a small, thin, man came into the room. He had evidently been eating his supper, because he was dabbing at his lips with a table napkin. "What can I do for you?" he asked.

"Are you the assayer?"

"Yes, sir, I'm Milton Bell," the little man replied.

Gid lay the saddlebags down on the counter, then opened the flap of one. Several thumb-sized rocks rolled out.

"I need you to take a look at this," Gid said.

Bell picked up a couple of rocks, looked at them casually, then put them down. He started to pick up another rock, but then put it down rather quickly and moved his hand to another instead. This rock drew considerably more interest than did the first two he had inspected. For this examination, he resorted to a magnifying glass.

"What do you think?" Gid asked. "Do I have anything here?"

"You might," Bell said, cautiously. He took a small pick from the drawer and began working on the rock, chipping off a piece of the color. Then he studied the color under the magnifying glass.

"Well?" Gid asked.

"It's going to take two, maybe three days before I have a final answer for you," Bell finally said.

"Why will it take that long?"

"I need to be sure," Bell replied. "Will you be staying in Gold Hill for long?"

Gid scratched his beard. "I had only intended to stay until I had a bath, a change of clothes, a meal, and a good night's sleep," he said. "I'm supposed to meet my brother over in Thornburg."

"You could send him a telegram," the assayer suggested.

"Yes, I could do that, I suppose," Gid replied. "But, why should I?"

"Trust me, it might well be worth your while," Bell said.

Gid thought of the welcome the two whores who had called down to him as he rode into town. "I might not

23

mind staying here a couple of days at that," he said.

The assayer took out a tablet, and picked up a pencil. "Now, what is your name, sir?"

"Crockett. Gid Crockett."

"Have you filed your claim?"

"I did a quick claim while I was up there," Gid said. "I made a pile of rocks, put my name and the date on a piece of paper, stuck the paper in an empty bean can, then buried it. I was told that was all I had to do. Was I told wrong?"

"No, sir, you did all that is necessary for a temporary claim," Bell said. "But for something more permanent, you will have to get your file on record. I can do that for you, if you will just fill out this form."

"You think all this is really necessary? I hadn't actually planned to do anything more permanent that scratch around a little and see if I could come up with a couple hundred dollars or so. I figured I would cash that in, then move on."

"Mr. Crockett, you are joking, aren't you?" Bell asked.

Gid cocked his head and looked at Bell with inquisitive eyes. "What are you trying to tell me, Mr. Bell?"

Bell took in the handful of rocks that had, thus far spilled from Gid's saddlebag. "Unless I am very, very wrong, I'd say you have at least a thousand dollars' worth of gold just in what you have brought in, in these saddlebags." He reached for the rock that had caught his particular interest a few minutes earlier, then put three or four more with it. "And if there are many more up there like these, you've got yourself a bonanza. Take my advice, Mr. Crockett. Fill out this form and get your claim registered."

"All right," Gid said, filling out the form Bell gave him. "You've talked me into it."

"Wait," Bell said, scribbling out a note. "If you are going to leave your ore here for me to look at more closely, you'll be needing a receipt." He handed the note to Gid.

"All this says is, received of Gid Crockett, fifteen pounds of mineral-bearing ore," Gid said. "What would keep you from giving me a sack of worthless rocks when I return?"

"I'm an honest business man, Mr. Crockett, and I would treat you fairly. However, under the circumstances, I don't resent your suggestion. It is good to be cautious." At the bottom of the receipt Bell wrote, "Estimated value of ore is one thousand dollars." He signed it, then handed it to Gid. "That's as good as money in the bank," he said.

"Money in the bank, huh? Do you think I could get anything for this note over at the bank?" Gid asked.

"I'm sure you could, but why would you give them any interest? In two or three days the assay will be complete and you can cash this out."

"You are too much the gentlemen to mention it, Mr.

Bell, but I need a bath and some clean clothes. I'd also like a decent meal and a place to sleep. Right now I don't have two coins to rub together."

Bell chuckled. "I understand," he said. "But I'm afraid the bank has already closed for the evening. However, if you don't mind giving me the interest, I'll lend you some money on this ore. How much do you need?"

"Can you go one hundred dollars?" Gid asked.

"I can do that," Bell said. On another piece of paper he wrote, "Received on ore, one hundred dollars cash," then he handed it to Gid to sign.

"That little piece you chipped off there," Gid said, pointing to the nugget. "How much is it worth?"

"Gold is forty dollars an ounce...this chip weighs six ounces, at least four ounces of which is gold....so, this would be one hundred sixty dollars."

"I'd like to keep that too, if you don't mind."

"Be my guest," Bell said, handing the small, peanut-shaped nugget to him.

"Guess I'd better tell my brother to join me here. Where is the telegraph office?" Gid asked.

"You'll find it down on the corner," Bell said. "Right next to the apothecary. I think he's closed for the night as well, unless it's an emergency."

"No, no emergency," Gid replied. "I'm just going to tell my brother to meet me here, is all. I can send it in the morning."

Chapter Four

Under the soft, golden light of three gleaming chandeliers, the atmosphere in The Desert Strike Saloon was quite congenial. Half a dozen men stood at one end of the bar, engaged in friendly conversation, while at the other end, the barkeep stayed busy cleaning glasses. Most of the tables were filled with cowboys, miners, and storekeepers laughing over exchanged stories or flirting with one of the several bar girls whose presence added to the agreeable atmosphere.

Because it was mid-June, the two heating stoves were now cold, though there continued to hang around these appliances the distinctive aroma of wood smoke from their winter's activity. Mixed with that scent were the smells of liquor, tobacco, women's perfume, and the occasional odor of men too long at work with too few baths.

Will's recent trip to Missouri was the longest the two

brothers had been separated since the war. With only each other to provide some sense of belonging, Will and Gid Crockett were nomads, moving through the West with no specific purpose and without any particular destination.

During the war, Will and Gid had ridden with Quantrill's Raiders, fighting in the bloody Kansas-Missouri border campaigns. Though they had also participated in the battles of Wilson's Creek and Shiloh as members of the regular Confederate Cavalry, their guerrilla activity with Quantrill was never forgiven. As a result, in some places of the country, they were still wanted men.

Unlike Frank and Jesse James, and the Younger brothers—colleagues during the war who had turned to the outlaw trail—Will and Gid had managed, for the most part, to avoid any direct conflicts with the law. However, though Will and Gid never looked for a fight, neither did they back away from one, be it with an outlaw or an overbearing peace officer. The very ferociousness with which they settled accounts had brought them a degree of notoriety.

At the moment, however, Will was enjoying the ambience of The Desert Strike Saloon. He was engaged in a game of stud poker with five players he had befriended, including the deputy sheriff, the doctor, and three of the more affluent merchants of the community.

To the casual observer it might appear that Will was so

relaxed as to be off guard. A closer examination, however, would show that his eyes were constantly flicking about, monitoring the room, tone and tint, for any danger. And, though he was engaged in convivial conversation with the others at the table, thanks to his keen sense of hearing, he was listening in on snatches of dozens of other conversations. Additionally, he possessed a sense that could not be described, a kinesthesis developed by years of exposure to danger.

"I believe it is your bet, Mr. Crockett," Jonah Pope said. Jonah was wearing the badge of a deputy sheriff.

Will looked at the pot, then down at his hand. He was showing one jack and two sixes. His down-card was another jack. He had hoped to fill a full house with his last card, but pulled a three, instead.

"Well?" Jonah asked.

It was easy to see why Jonah was anxious. The deputy had three queens showing.

"I fold," Will said, closing his cards.

Two of the other players folded and two stayed, but the three queens won the pot.

"Thank you, gentlemen, thank you," Jonah said, chuckling as he raked in his winnings.

"Jonah, you have been uncommonly lucky tonight," Doc Stevens said, good-naturedly.

"I'll say I have," Jonah agreed. "I've won almost a

month's pay."

"We'd better watch out, gentlemen, or Jonah will give up the deputy sheriffin' business and go into gambling, full-time," Doc said.

"Ho, wouldn't I do that in a minute if I wasn't married?" Jonah replied. "Another hand, boys?"

"Not for me," Will said, pushing away from the table and standing up. "I appreciate the game, gentlemen, but the cards haven't been that kind to me tonight. I think I'll just have a couple of drinks, then turn in."

"What's your hurry?" one of the businessmen asked. "Lurleen's too busy for you right now."

Lurleen was, at that moment, engaged in deep conversation with someone at the bar. Part of her job was to work the men for drinks, and she was very good at it because she had a good sense of humor. She had a way of making a man feel important around her, and she seemed to actually enjoy her time with the men...with any man.

"Well, she's a working girl," Will said easily. "She has to earn a living like everyone else."

Though Lurleen had been Will's particular favorite ever since arriving in Thornburg, he wasn't in the least possessive of her, nor did he ever exhibit any sign of jealousy when she was otherwise engaged. Will's easy attitude about his relationship with Lurleen had won friends among all the men. And, though Lurleen appreciated the fact that he held no animus toward her because of her job, somewhere, deep inside her, a tiny flame of regret flickered. She would never admit it, even to herself…but she sometimes wished he would show just a little jealousy.

"I hope you hear from your brother soon, Mr. Crockett," Doc said as Will left the table.

"Oh, I expect he'll be along in another few days," Will replied.

"Not too soon, I hope," Jonah teased. "I've enjoyed taking your money."

"I'm sure you have, Mr. Pope, I'm sure you have," Will said with a chuckle.

After a couple of drinks at the bar and a few flirtatious exchanges with one of the bar girls, Will went next door to the hotel, then upstairs to his room. He lit the lantern and walked over to the window to adjust it to catch the night breeze. That was when he saw a sudden flash of light in the hayloft over the livery across the street. He knew he was seeing a muzzle flash even before he heard the gun report, and he was already pulling away from the window at the precise instant a bullet crashed through the glass of the window and slammed into the wall on the opposite side of the room.

He cursed himself for the foolish way he had exposed himself at the window. He knew better.

There was another shot on the heels of the first, so

close to the first that Will was pretty sure there had to be two men shooting at him. But he had no idea who they were, or why they were trying to kill him. He reached up to extinguish the lantern.

"What was that?" someone shouted from down on the street.

"Gunshots. Sounded like they came from the ..."

That was as far as the disembodied voice got before two more shots crashed through the window. If Will thought the first two shots had cleaned out all the glass he was mistaken, for there was another shattering, tinkling sound of bullets crashing through glass.

"Get off the street!" Will heard a voice, loud and authoritative, floating up from below. "Everyone, get inside!"

Will recognized the voice. It belonged to Deputy Pope, the man with whom he had been playing cards but a few minutes earlier. On his hands and knees so as not to present a target, Will crept up to the open window.

"Jonah, stay away!" Will shouted down. He raised up just far enough to look through the window and saw Jonah heading for the livery stable with his pistol in his hand. "Jonah, no! Get back!"

Will's warning was too late. A third volley was fired from the livery hayloft, and Jonah fell face down in the street.

With his pistol in his hand, Will climbed out of

the window, scrambled to the edge of the porch, and dropped down onto the street. He ran to Jonah's still form, then bent down to check the deputy. Jonah had been hit hard, and through the open wound in his chest, Will could hear the gurgling sound of his lungs sucking air and filling with blood.

"Damnit, Jonah, I told you to get down," Will scolded softly.

"It was my job," Jonah replied in a pained voice. "Crockett...the money. See that Hannah gets my winnin's."

"I promise," Will said.

At that moment, two more rifle shots were fired from the livery. The bullets hit the ground close by, then ricocheted away with a loud whine. Will fired back, shooting once into the dark maw of the hayloft. Then, leaving Jonah, he ran to the water trough nearest the livery, and dived behind it as the assailants fired again. Both bullets hit the trough with a loud thocking sound.

Will could hear the water bubbling through the bullet holes in the water trough, even as he got up and ran toward the door of the livery. He shot two more times to keep the assailants back. When he reached the big, open, double doors of the livery, he ran on through so that he was inside.

"Where'd he go? Dixon, do you see him?" one of the men in the hayloft called.

"I think he come inside here," Dixon answered.

Will moved quietly through the barn itself, looking up at the hayloft just overhead. Suddenly he felt little pieces of hay falling on him and he stopped, because he realized that someone had to be right over him. Then he heard it, a quiet shuffling of feet. Will fired twice, straight up, then he heard a groan and a loud thump.

"That's six shots. You're out of bullets, you son of a bitch," a calm voice said. Will looked over to his left to see a man standing openly, on the edge of the loft. The man was holding a rifle and, inexplicably, he laughed. "I ought to thank you for killin' Dixon like you done. That just leaves more money for me." He raised his rifle to his shoulder, and Will fired.

"What?" the outlaw gasped in shock, dropping his rifle and clutching the wound in his stomach.

"You should have stayed in school," Will said flatly. "Maybe you would have learned to count." He watched as the man fell from the loft, flipping over so as to land on his back in the dirt below. Will walked over to look down at him.

"Crockett! Crockett, are you all right?" It was Sheriff Baxter's voice.

"I'm in here, Sheriff," he said.

Baxter came running in then, puffing from the exertion. He was holding his pistol and he looked down at the body.

"Poor Jonah's dead," Baxter said.

"Yeah, I was afraid of that," Will replied. He looked around. "What about the liveryman, Jasper?"

"Jasper's all right," Sheriff Baxter said. "He was down at The Black Kettle havin' his supper when all this started. Lucky for him the way bullets were flying all over the place."

"Yeah," Will replied. He nodded toward the body of the man he had just shot. "Do you know this fella?"

The sheriff rolled the body over with his foot and looked down at it. "I reckon I do. This is Albert Washburn," he said. "He's a saddle tramp who will do anything for money as long as it's illegal. He normally runs with a man named Dixon."

Will looked up. "That's the name I heard this one call out. You'll find Dixon up there."

"What were they after, do you know?"

"They were after me."

"You?"

Will sighed. "This one said that by killing Dixon, I had fixed it so he would get more money."

"Who's after you?"

"I have no idea, Sheriff. But I guess it could be about anyone. Truth to tell, my brother and I have put burrs under the saddles of more than a few hard hombres over the last several years."

Chapter Five

Gid Crockett wasn't sure what awakened him. It was not a slow return to consciousness for that was a luxury he couldn't afford. Too slow an awakening might mean he would never wake at all. Instinctively, he wrapped his hand around the butt of his pistol. It made no sound as he slipped it from its well-oiled holster.

Moonlight beamed in through the front window, casting indistinct shadows about the room. Gid stared through the shadows, toward where he knew the door to be. The blackness turned to gray as the door opened to reveal a woman. She was carrying a candle, and soft, golden light danced in the silk of her dress.

"Gid?" she whispered quietly.

"Yeah, I'm here," Gid replied. As he slid his pistol back into the holster, it glistened darkly in the ambient light.

"It's me, Molly. You said come on up at midnight."

Gid sighed and rubbed his eyes.

"You haven't changed your mind, have you?"

"No, I haven't changed my mind," Gid said. Molly was the friendlier of the two whores who had welcomed him into town when he arrived. After his bath and supper, he was more tired than he thought, and he asked her to give him a couple of hours of rest before she joined him. As he saw her standing there, her features softened by the light, he felt a stirring of interest, indicating that he was rested enough. "Come on in, close the door."

Molly stepped into the room, then closed the door behind her.

Molly was still asleep when Gid awoke the next morning. Leaving her in bed, he dressed, then went downstairs.

"Sir," the desk clerk called to him. "My night clerk reported that he saw a young woman go upstairs last night. He believes she went to your room."

"That's right," Gid replied.

The clerk cleared his throat. "Ladies and gents are not allowed in the same room if they aren't married,'" the clerk said sanctimoniously. "I'm afraid she'll have to leave, now."

"We aren't in the same room, because I'm not there," Gid said. "So, leave her alone."

Gid's resolute stare frightened the clerk.

The clerk swallowed a couple of times, realizing then that his throat had suddenly become very dry. "Uh, ve-very good sir," the clerk finally stammered. "I will allow her to awaken naturally."

"Good man," Gid said. "Now, who serves the best breakfast in town?"

"I believe that would be Little Man Keller's Cafe, sir, just down the street."

"Little Man Keller's," Gid said. "Thanks."

"You are quite welcome sir," the clerk said, looking up nervously toward the upstairs room where he knew a woman was being illegally domiciled.

Before going to breakfast, Gid stopped by the telegraph office to send a message to his brother. A sign on the counter said, "Western Union, Felix Crain, telegrapher."

"Good morning," Crain greeted Gid as he came in.

"Good morning, Mr. Crain," Gid replied, reading the sign. "I need to send a telegram."

"Well, you came to the right place," Crain joked. "If you had a toothache now, why, you would have to go next door to get a nostrum. On the other hand, anyone going next door to send a telegram would be out of luck." Crain laughed. "Do you want me to write it for you? Or can you write?"

"I can handle it," Gid said, taking the pad.

"Didn't mean any offense. There's lots of folks come

in here who can't write," Crain said.

"No offense taken," Gid said easily. Finishing his message, he slid the pad back to Crain. "How long before my brother will get this?"

"Why, no time at all, sir," Crain said. "They have a delivery boy in Thornburg, so, like as not, your brother will receive this at his breakfast."

"Thanks," Gid said, paying the rate.

From the telegraph office, Gid went directly to Little Man Keller's Café. The place was crowded with morning customers, but Gid found a table near the back. As he contemplated his order, he wondered how Will's trip to Missouri had been, though he didn't regret not going. There was nothing back there for them. Their parents were lying in graves, dug on land that was now being farmed by Yankees. The house in which Will and Gid had grown up was nothing but burnt timber and blackened chimneys. Relatives and friends were, for the most part, dead or scattered. There was little chance that anyone was still there. Still, Will wanted to go.

"Not me. I'm going prospecting," Gid said.

"Prospecting? Prospecting for what?" Will asked.

"I don't know. Gold or silver, I guess," Gid answered. "It's just somethin' I gotta do, Will. I mean, if I don't, I'll spend the rest of my life wondering if there was some big vein out there that I could've found, if I'd just made the effort to look for it. What do you say?"

Will laughed. "I tell you what, Little Brother. You go right ahead," Will said. Will called Gid 'Little Brother,' because Gid was the youngest, certainly not because of the relative size of the two men. In fact, Gid was forty pounds heavier and four inches taller than Will.

"And you don't mind going to Missouri by yourself?"

"I don't mind."

The owner of Little Man Keller's, who, by his size, was appropriately named, approached Gid's table with pad in hand. Though not quite a dwarf, Little Man was less than five feet tall.

"Yes, sir, what'll it be?" Little Man asked.

"You got any flapjacks?"

"Best in New Mexico."

"I'll take a dozen flapjacks," Gid said.

"A dozen?" Little Man asked in surprise. "That's a pretty big order. You sure you want that many?"

"Yes," Gid answered.

Little Man chuckled. "All right, friend, if you've got appetite enough to hold 'em, I'll sure cook 'em up for you."

Little Man started to turn, but Gid continued with his order.

"And a rasher of bacon, half-a-dozen sausage patties, and a big piece of fried ham," he added.

"Yes, sir," Little Man said, even more incredulous than before. Again, he started to turn, but Gid still wasn't finished.

"Better bring me a couple of eggs, over easy, a mess of grits..."

"I'm sorry, sir, we don't have any grits," Little Man said, interrupting Gid's soliloquy.

"No grits? All right then, bring me some fried potatoes, and uh...you got any gravy?"

By now Gid's rather prodigious order had attracted the attention of others near his table and nearly all conversation stopped as they listened in on his order.

"Yes sir, I've got gravy," Little Man said, astonished.

"Good, bring me a pan of biscuits and a side of gravy," Gid continued.

"Excuse me, sir. Where is all this food going?"

"Why, right here," Gid replied, as if surprised by the question.

"You're expecting company?"

Gid shook his head. "Not that I know of. But if someone joins me, be ready to increase the order, would you?"

"Increase the order, yes, sir," Little Man said, now in total disbelief. Little Man stood at Gid's table for several more seconds before he left.

"What is it?" Gid asked. "What are you waiting on?"

"I wasn't sure you were through with your order,"

Little Man said.

"That's it," Gid said, not picking up on Little Man's subtle sarcasm. "But you might check with me from time to time to see if I need anything else."

As Little Man headed for the kitchen, "to put on another shift," he teased, Gid thought about his brother. It would be good to see Will again, and to find out if there really was anyone left back in Missouri.

If everything went as it should, Will would be in Gold Hill this evening. Gid imagined that Will would be getting his message, just about now.

Chapter Six

Back in Thornburg at that very moment, a pan of phosphorous powder flashed as a photographer took a picture of Albert Washburn and Curley Dixon. The bodies of the two dead outlaws, their skin now a pale, blue-white, had been tied into their coffins and propped up against the front of the hardware store. Gus Thorsall, the photographer, was doing a booming business by charging citizens twenty-five cents apiece to be photographed standing next to the bodies. For an extra dime he would let them hold a pistol and pose as if they were the ones who had shot the outlaws.

The body of Deputy Jonah Pope was being treated with a little more respect. His last mortal remains now lay in repose in the parlor of his own house. His grieving widow was receiving visitors, some of whom had just come from the hardware store where they had gawked at the two men who had killed Jonah.

Earlier that morning, Will had given his own condolences to the widow, along with the ninety-four dollars in poker winnings Jonah had on him when he was killed. Now Will was in The Black Kettle restaurant, having breakfast.

Cautiously, a young boy came to his table. He was wearing a pair of gray, striped trousers, and a cap bearing the word "messenger."

"Mr. Crockett?" the boy said.

"Yes?"

"Telegram for you, Mr. Crockett."

"Thanks," Will said. He opened the telegram, then read it as he took a bite of his buttered biscuit.

"WIN. CAN'T COME TO THORNBURG NOW. YOU COME TO GOLD HILL. JOE."

"Will there be an answer, Mr. Crockett?" the messenger boy asked.

"Yes," Will answered. "Send this message. 'ON MY WAY'."

"'On my way,' yes, sir."

"Let's see, at ten cents a word, that'll be thirty cents," Will said. He started to hand the boy four dimes, three to pay for the message and one as a tip. Then he drew the fourth dime back and replaced it with a quarter. "Would you stop by the stable and tell Jasper to get my horse ready?"

"Yes, sir," the boy said, smiling broadly over his good fortune.

Will had a leisurely breakfast with Lurleen, then checked out of the hotel. Nothing in the telegram indicated he should hurry...just that he should come.

Lurleen waved goodbye to him, then returned to The Desert Strike. Although the saloon was open, there were only two customers in the place and they were the hard drinkers who cared nothing about ambience, girls, or even the quality of their liquor. They came here only to drink.

"Did you tell your friend good-bye?" the bartender asked as Lurleen passed by.

"Yes, unfortunately."

The bartender chuckled. "I thought you ladies were never supposed to get too interested in one customer."

"This one was different," Lurleen said.

Upstairs, Lurleen looked at herself in the mirror. She was wearing the same dress she had worn on the train when she first met Will. She put her fingers on her schoolmarm watch and looked at it for a moment. She felt depressed, not only because Will was gone, but because she realized that the life this watch and dress represented were gone too, and could never be reclaimed. With a sigh, she reached for the red satin dress with the daringly low-cut neckline and put it on her bed. This was who she was now.

When she heard the knock, she felt a sudden elation. Will had come back! Smiling, she hurried to the door.

It wasn't Will.

"I don't receive visitors until after six in the evening," she said. Turning away from him, she tried to close the door, but couldn't because her visitor put his foot in the way. "Who do you think you—?"

That was as far as Lurleen got. She suddenly felt strong hands around her neck. She tried to scream, but the crushed larynx prevented that. It also stopped her from breathing.

Will had been riding for eight hours. Behind him, like a line drawn across the desert floor, the darker color of hoof-churned earth stood out against the lighter, sunbaked ground. Before him, the desert stretched out in motionless waves, one right after another. As each wave was crested, another was exposed, and beyond that another still.

The ride was a symphony of sound: the jangle of the horse's bit and harness, the squeaking leather as he shifted his weight upon the saddle, and the dull thud of hoof beats.

He had filled the canteen before leaving Thornburg this morning. The distance between the two points was fifty miles, all of it through rugged, New Mexico desert.

The canteen was already down by a third, and he had been told that there were no dependable water holes between Thornburg and Gold Hill. Already, his tongue was swollen with thirst, but he allowed himself no more than one swallow of water per hour.

Squinting at the sun, he guessed that an hour had passed. He stopped his horse, mopped his brow, then reached for the canteen. He had just pulled the cork when the shot rang out.

The bullet hit his horse in the neck and blood gushed from the wound. Without a sound, the animal went down. Will jumped clear to avoid being pinned beneath it. As he did so, however, he dropped the canteen and water began running out onto the hot sand.

Will grabbed the canteen with one hand, while pulling his pistol with the other. He crawled over to his horse and, using it as a shield, looked around to see if he could spot his assailant.

He saw no one.

A moment later he heard the sound of a horse leaving at a gallop. Jumping up, he ran to a nearby rock out-cropping then climbed to the top. He saw a lone rider moving fast toward the south. Will aimed at him, then held his fire because the rider was already too far from him for a pistol shot.

Will hurried to his dead horse to get his rifle. The horse had fallen on the rifle and it took Will some time to get it free. By the time he was able to pull the Winchester from his saddle holster, the rider was too far away, even for a rifle. Despite that, Will took a shot at him, more out of frustration than any real hope of hitting him.

"Shit!" Will said, lowering the rifle when, as expected, he missed. "Who the hell is trying to kill me? And why?"

He sat down, puzzled by the sudden interest in having him killed. First, there was that incident back in Thornburg. And now, here. Even more puzzling was why the shooter didn't hang around and finish the job? He certainly had the advantage. Will was trapped here, without a horse and with only the water that was in his canteen.

At the thought of his canteen, Will hopped up from the rock and hurried over to check it. There was no sign of the spilled water, as it had already evaporated. He picked the canteen up and shook it, then groaned. It was down to one-half.

Will had a decision to make. He knew he had come at least twenty-five miles since he left Thornburg, which meant he had thirty-five miles to go to Gold Hill. Thornburg was east, Gold Hill was west. The man who had shot at him, however, had gone south. Why did he go south? Will tried to recall the last time he had checked a map. He was certain he had seen no settlement south of the line between Gold Hill and Thornburg. However, if one did exist, it would more than likely be on this side of the mountains, and they were only about fifteen miles away.

If he went south and there was another town, a town he knew nothing about, he would reach it in half the time it would take him to go to either Gold Hill or Thornburg. On the other hand, if he went south and there was no settlement, he would have lost his gamble, and, more than likely, he would die. Will didn't waste time deciding. He took a drink of water—not a swallow, a drink—then he corked his canteen and started south.

It was hard going. An hour or so into his walk, his feet began to swell inside his boots. He picked up needles from prickly pear and once he stumbled over a hedgehog cactus. As the day wore on, he began tiring, and he started breathing through his mouth. The hot, dry air created a tremendous thirst, and the more he thought about it, the thirstier he got. His throat grew more and more parched and his tongue swelled.

He tried to keep up the schedule of one swallow of water per hour, but he was working much harder now than he had been when he was riding, and it was nearly impossible to wait for an hour between swallows. In addition, there wasn't much water left.

Will had heard that a person could get water out of some types of cactus. He wasn't sure what kind of cactus would produce water. He thought saguaro would but he hadn't seen any. A couple of times he fired a bullet into the barrel of a cactus, then stuck his finger into the bullet hole to see if he could find any moisture. He did find a little moisture in one of them, and he started digging at the pulp, trying to pull the white, pasty substance through the bullet hole. As a result, he pierced his hands badly with the needles, but he did get a mouthful of wet pulp which he chewed. He also sucked his own blood.

He drank the last of his water at about five in the afternoon. He started to throw the canteen away, but decided to keep it in case he did stumble across a water hole somewhere.

Then, just before dark, a scattering of adobe buildings rose from the desert floor, wavering in the shimmering heat waves. The buildings so matched the desert in color and texture that at first Will wasn't even sure the town was there. Gathering what strength he had remaining, he started toward it. He had no choice, now. If it was real, he would live, if it was a mirage, he would die.

It took him another excruciatingly painful hour to reach the town. At the edge of town he stopped to catch his breath and read the sign:

WATSON

Pop. 256

"OBEY OUR LAWS OR PAY THE PENALTY."

Gathering his strength, Will staggered into the little town. Seeing a pump in the middle of town, he hurried toward it. He moved the handle a couple of times and was rewarded by seeing a wide, cool stream of water pour from the pump's mouth. Putting his left hand in front of the spout, he caused the water to pool and, continuing to pump, drank deeply. Never in his life had anything tasted better to him.

With the killing thirst satisfied, Will raised up from the pump and looked around the town. Just down the street a door slammed, and an isinglass shade came down on the upstairs window. A sign creaked in the wind and flies buzzed loudly around a nearby pile of horse manure.

These sounds were magnified because the street was silent. No one moved, and Will heard no human voice, yet he knew there were people around. There were horses tied here and there, three of them in front of a building which was identified by a sign as the Whistle Stop Saloon.

The thought of a cool beer seemed even more inviting to Will than the water, so he started toward it. Just before he got there, though, a man came out of the saloon and stood on the boardwalk.

"Where's your horse, Mister?" the man asked in a voice that sounded a little like a locomotive letting off steam.

"I left him dead in the desert," Will replied. He started

51

forward again, but the man was blocking his way.

"You walked into town?"

"Yes." Will was getting a little irritated. He was hot, tired, hungry, and badly in need of a beer. He didn't feel like explaining everything to this galoot.

The man who was blocking Will's way was a tall man, half a foot taller than Will, taller even than Gid. He was thin and muscular, with a moustache that curved up at each end, like the horns on a Texas steer. He was wearing a yellow duster, pulled back on one side to expose a long-barreled Colt sheathed in a holster that was tied halfway down the big man's leg. He had an angry, evil countenance, and looking directly at him was like staring into the eyes of an angry bull.

"Mister, you're in my way," Will said dryly.

"Would your name be Will Crockett?"

"It is. Why? Do you have a particular interest in me?"

"Yeah, I've got an interest in you." The big man pulled his yellow duster to one side and Will saw a peace officer's badge pinned to his shirt. "I'm arresting you for horse stealing."

"Horse stealing? What are you talking about? I don't even have a horse!"

"You come in here without a horse, that's true," the peace officer said. "But I figure you're plannin' on leavin' with one. So, let's just say I'm stoppin' a horse-stealin' before it takes place."

"Look, I've got no quarrel with the law," Will protested. "But I'm not going back out into that desert. I aim to get myself some supper and a couple of beers, then find someplace to spend the night. Tomorrow I'll buy a horse, then be on my way."

"I'll tell you where you can spend the night, in my jail. You aren't comin' in here."

Will curled his fingers. His hand was so painful and swollen from the frequent encounters with cactus needles that, if it came to a fight, he wasn't certain he could even make a fist. But he wasn't about to let this son of a bitch bully him out of town.

"Time's runnin' short," the lawman said. "What are you goin' to do?"

"I'm going to do just what I told you I was going to do," Will said, speaking slowly and dangerously. He pointed toward the saloon. "I'm going to go in there and get myself some supper and a couple of beers. Now, you can either step aside and let me by, or stay where you are while I come through you."

The lawman made his move then. Will had expected the lawman to use his larger size to try and enforce his order. To Will's surprise, however, the big man went for his gun.

The lawman was exceptionally quick for his size, and

his hand moved toward his long-barreled Colt as quickly as a striking rattlesnake.

Will was caught by surprise. As a result, he didn't even start for his gun until the lawman's gun was coming out. But if Will had been surprised by the sheriff's sudden draw, the sheriff was undoubtedly surprised by Will's speed. Will's draw was smooth and his practiced thumb came back on the hammer in one fluid motion.

In the final analysis, Will may have been given a slight edge by the fact that the Sheriff's gun had an extra-long barrel. He had not even cleared leather when Will's finger put the slightest pressure on the hair trigger of his Colt. There was a blossom of white, followed by a booming thunderclap as the gun jumped in his hand.

The sheriff tried to continue his draw but the .44 slug from Will's pistol caught him in the heart. When the bullet came out through the back, it brought half the sheriff's shoulder blade with it, leaving an exit wound the size of a twenty-dollar gold piece.

The sheriff's hand came away from his gun and it slipped back down into his holster as he staggered backward, crashing through the bat-wing doors, and backpedaling into a table before coming down on it with a crunch that turned the table into firewood. He landed flat on his back, on the floor, his mouth open and a little sliver of blood oozing down his chin. His body was still jerking a bit, but his eyes were open and unseeing. He was already dead, only the muscles continued to respond, as if waiting for signals that could no longer be sent.

Will bounded up onto the boardwalk, then pushed through the bat-wing doors, following the sheriff's body inside. A wisp of smoke curled up from the barrel of the pistol he still held in his hand.

There were a dozen people inside the saloon, caught by surprise at the sudden turn of events. They stood there, staring awestruck at the twitching giant of their lawman lying in the V of the broken table.

Not perceiving any immediate danger from anyone else in the room, Will put his pistol back in his holster.

"Mister, do you know who you just shot?" one of the men in the saloon asked.

"Afraid not," Will said. "We never got around to getting acquainted."

"His name is Ernest Townsend. Sheriff Ernest Townsend. Never figured anyone would be good enough to beat him."

"He didn't beat him," one of the others said. "Look there. The sheriff's gun is still holstered."

It had all happened so fast, that Will didn't realize Townsend's pistol had fallen back into the holster.

"He started his draw," Will said.

"Uh, huh. And you were so fast you killed him before

he could even get his hand to his gun. Is that what you want us to believe?"

"Believe it or not, it is the truth."

"You might be faster'n Townsend, but you ain't that much faster. No one is."

Will didn't like the way this was going, and he started to back out of the saloon. He had taken no more than two steps backward when he felt something cold and hard jam into his back.

"Mister, this here is a double-barreled Greener I'm holdin'," a voice said. "You make one move and I'm goin' to open you up like guttin' a hog."

"You men are making a mistake," Will said. "All I came here for is supper and a couple of beers." He nodded toward the Sheriff's body. "This fella threw down on me. I didn't have any choice."

"Let's hang the son of a bitch!" someone called.

"Yeah, somebody get a rope!"

"Hold on, hold on!" the man with the shotgun said. "Bein' as I was Ernest Townsend's deputy, I reckon I'm the sheriff now...leastwise, 'till we can get around to another election. And as the sheriff, I say they're ain't goin to be no lynchin'."

"This son of a bitch shot Ernest. You aim to just let him walk?"

"It just so happens that the judge is due here tomorrow.

I aim to try 'im, then hang 'im legal," the deputy said. He jabbed his shotgun into Will's back, poking him so hard that it nearly knocked the breath from him. "Come along, mister. We ain't that big a town, but we got us a fine jail, thanks to the man you just killed."

Gid was surprised when Will did not arrive that evening. He knew Will had received his message, because Will had answered him, and it wasn't like him to be late. After breakfast the next morning Gid waited anxiously for Will to show. A couple of times he checked the telegraph office to see if there were any messages for him, but nothing was there. When Will hadn't shown by noon, Gid began to worry.

Several scenarios passed through Gid's mind, and none of them were good. He knew Will wasn't lost. And he knew that Will wasn't still in Thornburg, for if he had been, he would have sent Gid another message explaining the delay. The most likely thing was that Will's horse had gone down on him. If so, Will would be facing a long walk, maybe with no water.

By one o'clock Gid had made up his mind. With two extra canteens of water hanging from his saddle pommel, he rode out of Gold Hill, headed for Thornburg.

One hour out of town, Gid saw something dark and ominous on the horizon. "Damn," he said aloud. "Get ready, horse. We're about to go through a sandstorm."

The sandstorm hit a few minutes later, and when it did, it hit with a terrible force. The wind howled like a thousand banshees and sand blew against him with such force that he felt as if it were going to tear his skin off. Tying his handkerchief around his horse's eyes, he led the terrified animal over to a small ridge. There, on the lee side, they waited for two hours until finally, the storm spent its violence.

The storm over, Gid resumed his journey. But, whereas before the storm, the desert had texture, now there was none. The desert floor was covered with smoothly rippled sand, much like an open field after a new snowfall.

It was nearly dark by the time Gid discovered the horse. Because of the drifting piles of sand, the animal was nearly buried and Gid almost didn't see it at all. There was no doubt about it being Will's horse. Gid recognized the saddle and tack.

A quick examination of the horse found the bullet wound that killed him. But he saw no other blood on the horse or saddle, so it gave him cause to hope that whoever shot the horse didn't shoot Will.

Gid looked through the saddlebags. He found a small packet of letters that Will was bringing back from Missouri. He read them and for a moment wished that he had gone back to Missouri with his brother. Though their parents had been killed during the war, their mother's sister was still alive and hers was one of the letters.

Also, Gid couldn't help but believe that if he had been with Will, none of this would have happened. Someone might have taken a shot at them, but together the Crockett brothers were so formidable as to be almost invulnerable.

Gid looked around for any sign of a trail. Normally he was a good tracker, better even than Will. But the sandstorm that just passed had completely obliterated any possible trail.

As far as Gid knew, there were two towns in this entire valley, Thornburg and Gold Hill. Since Will had not been in Gold Hill when he left and Gid didn't meet him on the trail, there was only one place he could be. When his horse went down, Will must have returned to Thornburg.

Putting the packet of letters in his own saddlebag, Gid remounted and started riding east.

Chapter Seven

"Breakfast," the deputy said.

Will sat up on the bunk and rubbed his eyes. The average man might have found it impossible to sleep while contemplating the thought of a murder trial and hanging, but Will wasn't the average man. He lived a life of such danger that the prospect of sudden death was always in his future. Also, he had arrived in Watson on the edge of exhaustion, so it had not been difficult for him to sleep that night.

"Thanks," Will said. He looked toward the tin plate the deputy slid through the door. It contained two biscuits.

"That's it? That's breakfast?"

"That and a cup of water," the deputy said.

Using a tin cup, the deputy scooped some water from a bucket, then passed it through the bars as well.

"Thanks."

There was a pot of coffee brewing on the stove and the deputy poured himself a cup, then looked back at Will.

After his long, dry day the day before, the water wasn't unwelcome. But the coffee smelled exceptionally good and he would have liked some. He would be damned before he asked for any though.

"Damn, this coffee is good this morning," the deputy said, smacking his lips in appreciation.

Will knew that the deputy was riding him, but he said nothing. Instead, he just returned to his bunk and began eating his biscuits and drinking his water.

The deputy tried a couple more times to get a rise from Will, but had no more success than he did with the coffee. Finally, he got up from his chair and walked over to look through the bars.

"What's it feel like to know you're goin' to die?" he asked.

"We're all going to die," Will replied. "It's just a matter of when. A hundred years from now, the worms will be finished with both of us."

The front door to the jail opened then, and a rather robust, bearded man wearing a suit came in. The deputy turned toward him, then smiled, broadly.

"Good mornin', Judge," he said. He pointed to the cell. "We got you a prisoner to be hung."

"We are going to try him first," the judge said. He

looked pointedly at Will. "Then we'll hang him."

"Yes, sir, that's what I meant to say," the deputy replied, his voice reflecting his toady deference.

The Judge walked over to the cell and looked through the bars at Will. "I am Judge Mason Huff," he said to Will. Then, over his shoulder, he called back to the deputy. "Mr. Lewis, do you know who we have here?"

"Who?" Lewis asked.

"We have Will Crockett of the Crockett brothers."

Will was surprised, not only that Huff knew he was a Crockett, but that he knew which one he was.

"No worse pair of murdering scoundrels have ever terrorized society," Huff said.

"Is that a fact? Is there a reward out for them?" Lewis asked excitedly. "'Cause, if there is, I caught 'im." The deputy hurried over to the desk, then started looking through all the reward posters.

"You won't find anything," Will said.

"He's right," Judge Huff said, turning away from the cell. "There are no dodgers out for the Crocketts. At least, none that I know of."

"I thought you said they was murderers," Lewis said.

"They are," Judge Huff insisted.

"How do you know that, if there ain't no posters out on them?"

"I know, because I know," Huff said. "What is today?"

"Today is Wednesday, June nineteenth," Lewis answered.

"All right, we'll hold the trial on Friday, the twenty-first. Haydon will prosecute. Woodward will defend."

"Woodward? You mean John Woodward? Judge, you're kiddin' ain't you?"

"I never 'kid,' Mr. Lewis. I assure you, I am quite serious. Where would Mr. Woodward be, right now?"

"More'n likely, he's sleepin' off last night's drunk some'eres," Lewis replied. "Prob'ly over in the livery. Dempsey lets him stay there sometimes."

"Get him. Tell him I will expect him in court this afternoon, prepared to defend this prisoner."

"Judge, ole' Woodward ain't drawed a sober breath in two years, let alone made an appearance in court. Ever since...."

"I'm well aware of John Woodward's travail," Huff said, interrupting Lewis in mid-sentence. "I realize things have not gone well for him of late. But as a qualified attorney, he has no choice but to accept this assignment, or I will jail him for contempt of court and disbar him for life."

"You're goin' pretty harsh on him, ain't you, Judge?"

"Just find him," Judge Huff ordered.

John Woodward awakened to the smell of horse manure. He was used to the smell, sleeping in the livery as often as he did, but this morning it seemed much stronger than usual. When he opened his eyes, he saw why. Too drunk last night to realize what he was doing, he had gone to bed in a pile of the stuff. It was all over him, and he began scraping it off.

"Woodward? Woodward, you in here?"

"I'm back here," Woodward replied.

Deputy Lewis came back to him, then stopped several feet away. "Son of a bitch!" Lewis gasped. "Damn, you stink." He waved his hands in front of him.

"Yes, well, I wasn't all that particular about where I slept last night," Woodward answered. "What is it, Deputy? What do you want?"

"I don't want nothin'. It's the judge that wants you."

"Judge Huff?"

"Yeah, he's over to the sheriff's office now. He wants you to defend a prisoner."

Woodward shook his head. "I don't practice law any more, Judge Huff knows that."

"That may be but he asked me to find you."

"Very well, Mr. Lewis, you have found me. Now, go back and tell the judge that I have no intention of trying a case in my present condition."

"You got to," Lewis said. "The judge said if you don't, he'll throw you in jail for contempt, then have you dis... dis...something or the other."

64

"Disbarred?"

"Yeah, I think that's what he said."

"Yes, that sounds like something Judge Huff would do." Woodward looked down at himself. "I can't see the judge looking like this."

"He didn't say nothin' 'bout how you was s'posed to look. He just said fetch you back to him, and that's what I aim to do."

Woodward scraped off as much of the greenish-brown goop as he could, then nodded at the deputy. "All right," he said. "Let's go see the distinguished jurist."

"The what?"

"Judge Huff," Woodward said.

"Yeah, let's go. Only, stay upwind of me."

Huff took one look at and one whiff of John Woodward then ordered him to take a bath and get on clean clothes before presenting himself.

"It costs a quarter to take a bath," Woodward said. "And three dollars to get my clothes out of the boarding house. Missus Sutherland is holding them in lieu of my bill."

"I'm authorizing payment of twenty dollars to serve as public defender," Judge Huff said. "Here's five dollars in advance. Come back when the smell of you doesn't sicken a pig."

"Yes, sir," Woodward mumbled.

Lewis chuckled as Woodward left. "Hey, Crockett, did you see that man?" he called.

"See him? For a moment, I was afraid he would be sharing a cell with me," Will answered.

"Sharing your cell? No, it's better than that," Lewis said. "Woodward is a lawyer. Fact is, he's your lawyer." Lewis whooped with laughter.

When a well-dressed and rather dignified man stepped into the sheriff's office an hour later, Lewis didn't recognize him.

"Yes, sir, something I can do for you?" Lewis asked.

"Don't you recognize me, Deputy? It is I, John Woodward."

Lewis's eyes grew wide. "Well, I'll be damned. It is you," he said.

Woodward nodded toward the cell. "I would like to speak with my client."

"Sure, go right ahead."

"Alone," Woodward said.

"Alone? What do you need to see him alone for? Hell, just go over there and talk to the son of a bitch."

"Article fifteen, paragraph six, slash, b of the New Mexico law code says that defense council will be given a room to have private consultations with their clients. Since you have no such place, that means you must step outside," Woodward said.

"To hell with that. There ain't no drunk goin' to tell me what I got to do."

"I can get a court order from Judge Huff to order you to do so," Woodward said.

Lewis glared at Woodward for a moment, then, with a sigh, took his hat down from the peg and jammed it onto his head.

"All right," he said. "I'll give you your time." He nodded toward the street. "I'll just be out there if you need me."

"Thank you, Deputy. I won't be needing you," Woodward said.

Lewis nodded once, then looked back toward the cell and Will.

"All right, Crockett. Here's your lawyer. Better talk fast, while he's still sober." Lewis laughed at his own joke as he stepped outside.

Woodward went over to the stove and with shaking hands, poured himself a cup of coffee. Then, without being asked, he poured a second cup and carried it over to the cell to pass between the bars. His hand was shaking so that some of the coffee was splashing out.

"Better get it while there's some left in the cup," Woodward said, making a bitter joke at his own expense.

"Thanks," Will replied.

Woodward pulled a chair over and sat down, just

outside the cell. He studied Will over the rim of his cup as he took another swallow. "They didn't tell me your name," he finally said.

"Crockett. Will Crockett."

"Mr. Crockett, I'm John Woodward...and I am your court-appointed attorney."

"My court-appointed attorney?"

"That's right, sir. Of course, you don't have to accept me. You can hire your own."

"Are there any other attorneys in this town?"

"Only one, and he will be prosecuting," Woodward replied.

"Are you really an attorney?"

"Yes, sir, I am, duly qualified before the bar."

"You'll forgive me for asking, but when I saw you earlier, you didn't exactly look like a lawyer," Will said.

"That is very true. I have been besieged by demons, as it were, for some two years now. But I assure you, I am a qualified lawyer, and I will do all I can for you. Now, if I may ask, with what crime are you charged?"

Will looked at Woodward in surprise. "You are my lawyer and you don't even know that?"

"I know nothing about you or the charge, Mr. Crockett," Woodward replied. "My introduction to this case occurred approximately an hour and a half ago when Deputy Lewis pulled me from a pile of horse shit where I had spent the night." Woodward looked around the office. "By the way, where is Sheriff Townsend? I haven't seen him yet."

"Well, you've asked two questions," Will said. "But I can answer both of them at the same time. The reason Townsend isn't here is because he is dead. And the reason I am here, is because I am the one who killed him."

Woodward had been slouching in the chair. He sat up quickly when Will said he had killed Townsend. The expression on his face was one of shock.

"You killed Townsend? How?"

"He braced me as I was going into the saloon last night," Will said. "We had a few words and the next thing I knew, he was going for his gun. I had no choice but to kill him."

"You say he was going for his gun, but you still managed to shoot him?"

"Yes."

Woodward shook his head. "Mister, you are either incredibly fast or a bold-faced liar. And it doesn't make any difference which one you are because the jury is never going to believe anyone was able to beat Sheriff Townsend on the up and up."

"What about you? Do you believe me? I mean, if you are going to be my lawyer, you have to believe me, don't you?"

"No, sir, I don't have to believe you to represent you,"

Woodward said. "But I understand now why Judge Huff chose me to defend you."

"Why?"

"It is Huff's penchant for irony, Mr. Crockett," Woodward said as he got up and walked back over to the coffee pot to refill his cup. Using both hands to steady his cup, he took another drink. "Yes, sir, I imagine he is having quite a laugh over this...as is Townsend...if there is such a thing as laughter in hell," he added.

Chapter Eight

Gid's first stop when he reached Thornburg was the telegraph office.

"Yes, sir, you want to send a telegram?" the telegrapher asked, stepping up to the counter. He was a small, bald man who kept his thick glasses on by way of a black ribbon which stretched from earpiece to earpiece around the back of his head.

"No, thanks," Gid answered. "But I'm looking for someone who has recently sent a telegram from this office. His name is Will, and he stands about this high." Gid held his hand out four inches below the top of his own head. "Weight wise, I'd say he dresses out around a hundred and eighty pounds or so. His hair is light and his eyes are blue."

"Mister, you don't have to describe Will Crockett to me, or to anyone else in this town," the telegrapher replied. "Not after what happened Saturday night."

"What happened?"

For his answer, the telegrapher slid a copy of the local newspaper across the counter.

GUNFIGHT HURLS THREE MEN TO ETERNITY

Deputy Jonah Pope Killed, His Widow Mourns

Albert Washburn and Curley Dixon Also Slain

World is Better Off for Their Demise

Saturday night, at fifteen minutes of eleven o'clock, the streets of Thornburg became a battlefield when four desperate men threw themselves at each other in mortal struggle. At last, when the smoke had cleared, only one, Will Crockett, remained alive. By his courage, and the accuracy of his shooting, the murder of Deputy Jonah Pope was avenged, and two of the most pernicious desperadoes ever to walk the streets of Thornburg were dispatched to their Maker, whose mercy they can only hope for, as no one who remains on this mortal coil would deign to lift a prayer on their behalf.

Gid read the article, then looked up from the paper.

"Yes," he said. "That would be Will. Do you know where I can find him?"

"You won't find him in Thornburg. He has gone over to Gold Hill to meet his brother," the telegrapher said.

"I am his brother, Gid. And I did send a telegram asking him to come. He answered that he was on his way, but he never got there."

The telegrapher clucked his tongue and shook his head. "Oh, dear," he said. "The country between here and Gold Hill is most inhospitable. I do hope nothing bad has happened to him."

"I thought perhaps he might have come back to Thornburg," Gid said. He didn't tell the telegrapher about finding Will's horse.

"Well, if he did, you might ask Mr. Bailey. He's the clerk at the Saint Albans Hotel. That's where he was staying."

"Thanks," Gid said.

The Saint Albans Hotel was bracketed by two saloons, O'Reilly's on the right and The Desert Strike on the left. If he found out nothing at the hotel, he would ask in the saloons.

There was a small lobby just inside the door of the hotel. The lobby was furnished with one, well-worn, horsehair sofa and a scarred rocking chair. A brass spittoon occupied the space between the chair and the sofa. A threadbare carpet covered the floor. In the corner was a cast-iron stove, cold now, in the summer months. The smokestack was removed and the flue cover on the chimney was decorated with a painting of bright, red flowers.

To the right of the door as he came in was a counter

that divided the lobby from the office area. On the left wall just beside the counter was a cabinet of cubbyholes, each hole containing the room key. One or two of the cubbyholes had envelopes in them. The back wall was dominated by a large clock, its face divided by Roman numerals. The pendulum swung in a measured arc, each movement emitting a loud tick-tock.

The hotel clerk was not wearing a jacket. The long sleeves of his striped shirt were gathered with garters, just above the elbows. Wearing a bolo tie and bright orange suspenders, he was eating an apple as he stepped up to the desk.

"You would be Bailey?"

"I am, sir. What can I do for you?"

"I need to see your guest book," Gid said. "I'm looking for Will Crockett."

"Mr. Crockett stayed with us for nearly a week, but he checked out Sunday morning."

"And you're sure he didn't come back?"

"I'm positive he didn't come back. I would have known."

"Is there another hotel in town?"

"We are the only hotel of any consequence," Bailey said smugly.

"Thanks," Gid said, disappointed. His hope had been that somehow Will had made it back to Thornburg. It appeared that Will hadn't come back at all. Or if he had, he had not returned to the hotel.

"Will you be wanting a room, sir?" the clerk asked.

Gid hadn't come to the hotel with the intention of taking a room, but it was too late to do any more traveling that night, so the idea suddenly sounded good to him. "Yes," he said. "Yes, I believe I will take a room."

"Very good sir. And your name?"

"Crockett. Gid Crockett."

"You are related to Mr. Will Crockett?"

"He's my brother," Gid explained. "We were supposed to meet in Gold Hill, but he never showed."

"I can understand now, your interest in him," the clerk said. He nodded toward one of the saloons. "If it is of any help to you, Mr. Crockett, he spent a good deal of time in one of the saloons. As I recall, he seemed to prefer The Desert Strike."

"Thanks," Gid said. He paid for the room, but didn't go up right away. Instead, he went next door to The Desert Strike to follow up on the lead.

As far as small town saloons went, Gid thought The Desert Strike was fairly nice-looking. It sported a real mahogany bar. A mirror behind the bar was bracketed by a shelf that was filled with scores of bottles of various kinds of liquor and spirits. A sign on the wall read: "Gentlemen, kindly use the spittoons."

"What'll it be, gent?" the bartender asked, sliding down

the bar with a towel tossed across his shoulder. The fact that the towel was relatively clean, spoke volumes about the class of the establishment.

"Beer," Gid replied. "Do you serve eats?"

"Bacon, beans, biscuits," the bartender replied.

"I'll take it," Gid said. Scooping a couple of boiled eggs from the large jar that sat on the end of the bar, Gid took them and his beer over to a nearby table. It didn't take long for one of the bar girls to approach him.

"Hello," she said, smiling her greeting at him. "My name is Suzy."

Suzy was tall, raw-boned, and full-breasted. She had wide set, blue-gray eyes, high cheekbones, and a mouth that was almost too full. She was the kind of woman that Gid found most desirable, and of all the bar girls present, she was the one who left the pack to greet him. It was as if such women had a sixth sense about them, as if they intuitively knew they were the kind of girl he was attracted to.

"I don't think I've seen you in here, before," Suzy said.

"Just got into town," Gid answered. He kicked a chair out by way of invitation, then nodded at the bartender. The bartender brought Gid a second beer, as well as a drink for the girl, even though the girl hadn't ordered.

"He must know your brand," Gid said.

"One glass of tea is pretty much like any other glass of

tea," Suzy said with unaccustomed candidness. She picked it up and held it toward Gid in a toast. He laughed, then touched his beer to her glass.

"Well, at least you're honest about me paying whiskey prices for your tea."

"Honey, if everything we drank really was whiskey, we'd all be soused by seven every night," Suzy explained. "And what good is a soiled dove if she's passed out drunk?"

Gid laughed. "I can see your point," he said.

"So, what brings you to Thornburg?" Suzy asked.

"I'm looking for someone."

"Seems like everybody is looking for someone or something," Suzy said. "Who are you looking for?"

"I'm looking for my brother, Will Crockett."

"You're Will's brother? Then you must be Gid."

"You know him then? I see that I came to the right place."

"You came to the right place, all right. I'm glad to see that the two of you came back. Especially after what happened. Are you supposed to meet him in here?"

Gid shook his head. "We didn't come back."

Suzy looked confused. "What do you mean? You're here, aren't you?"

"I am, but Will isn't. He never showed over in Gold Hill. When I came back along the trail looking for him, I found his horse, dead. But there was no sign of my brother. He didn't go on to Gold Hill, and now it looks like he didn't come back this way, either."

"Couldn't you track him?"

Gid shook his head. "Afraid not. A big sand storm came up and blew away all the tracks. By the way, what do you mean after what happened?"

"With Lurleen."

"Lurleen?"

"Lurleen took a particular shine to your brother, and I think he liked her."

"Where is she? I would like to talk to her."

"Just a minute," Suzy said. She walked over to the bar and said something to the bartender. The bartender nodded, then reached under the bar and came up with a newspaper, which he handed to Suzy. Suzy brought the paper back to the table.

"Maybe you should read this," she said, handing the paper to Gid.

"Yes, the telegrapher showed me the story about the shooting that Will was in. I've read it."

"No," Suzy said. "Not that story. This story." She pointed to another story at the bottom of the page.

WOMAN FOUND STRANGLED
Lurleen Simpson Killed in Her Room
Sheriff Baxter Has No Suspects

Lurleen Simpson, a popular soiled dove who plied her avocation at The Desert Strike Saloon, was found strangled in her room on Saturday last. She was last seen alive at about eight thirty that morning by George Kuntz, the bartender at The Desert Strike and by two customers.

Although Sheriff Baxter has no suspects, he believes robbery may have been the motive. A broach watch, which belonged to Miss Simpson, has not been found. It is thought that the killer may have strangled her, then took the watch as payment for his grizzly deed.

"It says here that there are no suspects," Gid said as he finished the article. "Has the sheriff come up with anyone since the article was written?"

Suzy shook her head. "You know, when someone goes into 'the life', real people forget all about us. In many cases, even our families turn their backs on us. So, when something happens to one of us, like what happened to Lurleen, it doesn't mean much. Nobody cares about a dead whore."

"That's not true," Gid replied. "If Will knew about this, he would care. I care and I never even met her."

"You and your brother are exceptions then," Suzy said. "I hope you find your brother, but his chances aren't very good, are they? I mean, if you found his horse dead, that means he's on foot, wandering around out in the desert."

"The chances aren't good for an ordinary man. But Will's not an ordinary man, so I'm not ready to count him out, yet."

As he ate his supper, Suzy told Gid all she knew about Will. She pointed out some of the men with whom Will had played cards and, after his supper, Gid talked to them as well.

All wanted to share the story of Will's participation in the shoot-out that some insisted would make Thornburg famous. But no one was able to shed any light on anything that may have happened to Will. They did express some concern over the fact that Will had lost his horse during the trip.

"The desert between here an' Gold Hill ain't where a man on foot needs to be," one of them said.

None of the men even mentioned Lurleen Simpson, giving some credence to Suzy's comment that nobody cares about a dead whore.

Gid left The Desert Strike at about nine-thirty, then went over to O'Reilly's to check it out. O'Reilly's was a saloon that catered to the rougher trade. It had none of the niceties of The Desert Strike, no tables, no mirror behind the bar, and no girls. The bar itself was made of rip-sawn, unpainted pine. The drinks were cheaper, and the whiskey raw. Gid didn't have to hang around there. He knew this wouldn't be one of Will's regular haunts.

When Gid stepped back out into the street, he felt the impact of the bullet before he heard the shot. He was hit in the side, and drawing his own gun, he turned and looked into the dark shadow between the buildings. He heard running feet, but saw nothing.

Gid felt the nausea rise up in him. Bile surged in his throat. Dizzy, he staggered over to The Desert Strike, then went back inside. All conversation stopped at his entrance, and the silence lingered like a leaden weight over Gid's head. Everyone stared at him with curiosity. This time, their mouths opened in shock.

Gid didn't realize it, but he was quite an apparition to behold. He stood there, just inside the swinging bat-wing doors, ashen-faced, holding his hand over a wound which spilled bright-red blood between his fingers. He surveyed the room for just a moment, then, with effort, walked to the bar.

"Whiskey," he ordered.

The solemn-faced bartender poured him a glass and Gid took it, then turned around to face the silent patrons. By now his side was drenched with blood from his wound, and the blood was beginning to soak into the wide-planks of the floor.

"Gid!" Suzy called out in alarm, moving to him quickly. Gid held his hand out to keep her away.

"If any of you had anything to do with me getting shot,

I'm going to give you fair warning. The next man who even looks at me cross-eyed, I'm going to pull him apart with my bare hands." Gid looked at them, tossed down the drink, then set the empty glass on the bar. After that, he walked calmly from the bar. With each passing moment, he was growing more dizzy and more light-headed from the loss of blood. When he reached the entrance to the saloon, he stuck out one hand to grab the door frame. He struggled to steady himself as he walked out of the saloon.

Gid started toward the hotel, only this time he moved far enough away from the buildings so that there was no chance of anyone else jumping him from the shadows. He moved out into the middle of the street and lurched along with a stumbling, staggering gait, trying to stay on his feet, though his head was now spinning so badly he could barely stand.

When he finally reached the front of the hotel he fell against the door, managing to keep on his feet, then stumbled through. He knew he had to get off his feet quickly, so he lurched toward the stairs to keep from falling on the floor.

"Mr. Crockett!" Bailey called, startled by Gid's unusual entry. "Mr. Crockett, are you all right?"

"I'm fine," Gid said. "I'm just fine."

Gid leaned against the wall beside the stairs for a moment to get his breath, and when he did so, he left a stain of his blood. Then, holding his side, he climbed the stairs to his room. Feeling the wound, he realized that the bullet had passed all the way through him. That was good. He knew that if the bullet was still inside, it would be much more dangerous.

Gid ripped the bed sheet in two and wrapped it around his side, pressing it tightly against both the entry and the exit wounds. When the crude bandage was in place, he fell across the bed, closed his eyes and passed out cold.

Chapter Nine

John Woodward was just finishing his meeting with Will, when the man Judge Huff had chosen to act as prosecutor arrived. Haydon swept into the sheriff's office, dressed in tails and a stove-pipe hat, while carrying a silver-headed cane. He wore a diamond stickpin in his cravat and silver links at his cuffs. A gold watch chain stretched across the silk vest, accenting his rather considerable girth. His hair was neatly trimmed, as was his Van Dyke beard.

"Good morning, Mr. Woodward," Haydon said.

"Good morning, Mr. Haydon."

"May I interview the prisoner? Or do you require a little more time?"

"He's all yours," Woodward said, starting toward the door.

"You are welcome to stay while I talk to him," Haydon said. He put his cane and stove-pipe hat on the sheriff's desk.

"Thank you, no, I...uh...have some business to attend to."

"To be sure. Well, you go right ahead, Mr. Woodward," Haydon said.

"Woodward," Will called as Woodward started through the front door. Woodward turned back toward him. "Will you be sober when I see you next?"

"A good question," Woodward replied. "And under the circumstances, you are entitled to an honest reply. Well, here it is, Mr. Crockett. It is certainly my intention to be sober when you see me next, and I am going to try. But I can't promise you."

Will nodded. "If I can't have sobriety, Mr. Woodward, then I will settle for honesty," he said.

Haydon chuckled as Woodward left the office. "You may just have given him permission to get drunk again."

"Mr. Woodward is an adult," Will replied. "If he wants to get drunk, he certainly doesn't need my permission."

"To be sure, to be sure," Haydon said. He cleared his throat. "Mr. Crockett, my name is Oscar Haydon, and I am here to prosecute you. I don't suppose there is any need in telling you that you are in a great deal of trouble."

"I sort of figured that out," Will said.

"You can save yourself some trouble by confessing."

"Confessing what? That I killed Townsend? Hell, I did kill him."

"I mean confessing that you drew first, that there was no gunfight as you claimed, and that you killed him with malice and aforethought. Come clean with that, Mr. Crockett, and you could save us all a lot of trouble."

Will chuckled. "What about the hangman? Would I save him trouble as well?"

Haydon shook his head. "Since you prize honesty so, I'll be honest with you. The only trouble you will save, is the trouble of a trial. There is no plea bargain being offered. I'm afraid Judge Huff plans to hang you, no matter what."

"Then I may as well stick to my story."

"Let me get this straight. Your story is that Townsend started to draw on you...whereas you, seeing the sheriff start his draw, commenced your own draw, and beat him. And, you not only beat him, you were so fast that when he came crashing backwards through the door into the saloon his pistol was still in its holster. Is that about it?"

"That's it," Will said.

Haydon clucked his tongue and shook his head. "Mr. Crockett, do you have any idea how ridiculous that claim is? Townsend was, by all accounts, incredibly fast with a gun. Now...while it is possible that someone may have been faster—perhaps even you—it is highly unlikely that anyone would be so much faster that Townsend's gun would still be sheathed."

"It doesn't look good, does it?" Will asked.

"No, sir, it doesn't look good at all. As a matter of fact, it is the most far-fetched thing I could possibly imagine."

"Nevertheless, that is what happened," Will insisted.

"So, you are sticking by your story?"

"I reckon I don't have any choice since what I'm saying is true," Will said.

Haydon walked back over to the sheriff's desk and picked up his hat and cane. He put his hat on his head, then squared it, before he turned to look back toward Will in the jail cell.

"Have it your way, Mr. Crockett," Haydon said. "It was my intention to spare you the indignity and humiliation of a public trial, but you spurned my offer."

Will laughed. "The indignity and humiliation of a public trial? You just told me the judge plans to hang me no matter what. What could be more undignified and humiliating than a public execution?"

"I'll see you in court," Haydon said. "Good day, Mr. Crockett."

After Haydon departed, Will stood at the bars of his cell for a moment, looking over the empty room, studying every aspect of it. Directly across from him, and running parallel with the cell, was the front wall. The door was in the center of the wall, with a window on either side of the door. The windows were dirty, with half their openings masked by window shades of dark green. The wall to his right had another window, and a large board to which were posted dozens and dozens of Wanted Posters.

The poster board was obviously not kept up-to-date, for Will recognized one of the wanted men as someone he had killed more than two years earlier. As he studied the other posters, he realized that he had run across several of the others as well, for both Will and his brother lived the kind of lives that brought them in frequent contact with such men.

There was also a calendar on the wall. The picture on the calendar was of a passenger train, roaring through the night with sparks spewing from the smokestack and steam streaming from the cylinder. Every window of every car was glowing with light.

On the calendar page, every day had been X'd out until the current day, which was Wednesday, June nineteenth. Will heard the Judge say he wanted the trial to be held on the twenty-first. He couldn't help but wonder if he would still be alive by the twenty-second.

Where was Gid? Was he still waiting for him in Gold Hill? Knowing Gid, Will doubted very much if he was. Gid had probably come looking for him and, if so, would have found, not only his horse, but his tracks leading here. Gid would find him, Will was certain of that. Gid could track a fish through water.

As Will stood at the bars of his cell, musing over his situation, the front door opened again. Hesitantly, a young woman stuck her head through the door.

"Deputy Lewis?" she called.

"He isn't here," Will said.

"Are you Will Crockett?" the girl asked.

"Yes."

Nervously, the girl brushed a fall of hair back from her forehead and walked over to the cell. Although she was a blonde, her eyes were deep brown. It was an unusual and very attractive combination. "Would you come closer, please?" she asked.

Will, who was already standing next to the bars, wondered just how much closer he could get. She answered his question for him when she stuck her arm through the bar, put her hand on the back of his neck, and pulled his face toward her. Through the bars, she kissed him full on the mouth.

Will was startled by the young woman's unexpected move but it wasn't at all an unpleasant surprise.

When she pulled away from him she looked up at him with her large dark eyes.

"Thank you," she said.

"One little kiss isn't much to thank a man for," Will replied. "If I ever get out of here, maybe I can do something that really earns your thanks."

For just a moment the girl looked baffled, then suddenly she laughed.

"I wasn't thanking you for the kiss," she said. "The kiss was my way of thanking you."

Now it was Will's time to be confused. "Thanking me for what?" he asked.

Will had never seen anyone's face transformed as quickly as did the young woman's. The smile left her lips and her eyes narrowed with loathing.

"For killing Ernest Townsend," she said.

"Yes, well, I'm glad it earned your approval," Will said. "But I have to tell you, it wasn't anything I planned. It just happened."

"I don't care how it happened. As long as he is dead."

"Even if I hang for killing him?"

Before the girl could answer, the front door to the jail opened and John Woodward came in. He was carrying a couple of books with him, and when he saw the girl, he looked surprised.

"Nora, what are you doing here?"

"I came to thank Mr. Crockett for doing what nobody else in this town had the courage to do."

"He needs more than thanks," Woodward said.

"Put me on the stand," Nora said. "Let me tell my story."

Woodward shook his head no. "That would only complicate things," he said. "Mr. Crockett claims that

Townsend drew first. If you tell your story, it might suggest to the jurors that Crockett planned to kill Townsend. It could even plant the idea that you paid him to kill Townsend."

"I would have paid him to kill Townsend. I would have paid anyone to kill him, if I had thought I could find such a person."

Woodward nodded. "Uh, huh. Do you see what I mean? Believe me, having you take the stand would only make matters worse. Let the court handle it."

"That's what you told me two years ago."

Woodward nodded. "It wasn't the court who failed you then, darlin'. It was me."

"If that's true, you can make it up to me now," Nora said.

"How?"

Nora looked back toward Will. "Get this man off," she said.

Woodward held up one of the two books he was carrying. "I've been working on that," he said. "I may have found a way to keep him from hanging."

Nora shook her head. "I don't mean just keep him from hanging," she said. "I mean, get him off. I want him to go free."

"You're asking for a miracle," Woodward said.

"You owe me a miracle," Nora replied coldly.

Chapter Ten

Shortly after Gid staggered out of The Desert Strike, Suzy went into the kitchen of the saloon where a medical kit was kept. She got a roll of bandages, some salve and crushed aloe leaves, then sneaked out the back door, and down the alley, to the back of the hotel. Slipping in through the back door of the hotel, she walked quickly through the hallway until she reached the lobby. Bailey was reading the Gazette. He looked up when Suzy came in.

"Hello, Suzy. Do you have business over here tonight?" Bailey asked. He looked at her lustfully. He had once offered her a deal. He would make a room available for her for any business she might want to conduct "off the books" of the saloon. In return, she would provide him with her services.

Suzy declined the offer, but Bailey never stopped thinking about the possibilities.

"No. I just stepped out for some fresh air and I thought I would come in and say hello to you. It's been a while since you stopped by for a drink."

"Yes, well, uh, Mrs. Bailey doesn't really approve," Bailey said.

Suzy leaned over the counter, affording him a magnificent view of her cleavage. When his eyes went there, as she knew they would, she managed to reach around the corner and take the skeleton key from its hook. With that key she could open any door in the hotel.

"Oh, that's such a shame," Suzy said. "The girls all enjoy your company so. One of them asked me just the other day if I thought you would ever come back."

"Really? Which girl?" Bailey asked, his voice dripping with lust.

"I think it was Pearl," Suzy said. There was no girl named Pearl, but Bailey didn't know that.

"Pearl, yes! Tell her...tell her I'll be by to see her soon," Bailey said excitedly.

"I'll do that. Well, I must go back to work. Goodbye."

"Goodbye, Suzy," Bailey said.

Suzy had accomplished two things by her conversation with Bailey. Out of the corner of her eye, she had checked the register to see that Gid Crockett was in room 201. And, she had managed to secure the pass key.

Suzy walked back to the front door. She opened it,

then looked back at Bailey, who had already returned to the Gazette. She closed the door, then stepped behind a large, potted plant. Studying Bailey through the leaves, she waited until he got up and walked to the back of his office to pour himself a cup of coffee. That gave her the opportunity she was looking for, and she slipped quickly and quietly up the stairs to the landing on the second floor.

A moment later, she was slowly and quietly letting herself into Crockett's room. With her heart pounding fiercely for the risk she was taking, she closed the door behind her, then stood for a moment in the dark shadows, letting her eyes adjust to the darkness.

The room was hot and sticky, and she could smell the blood from Gid's wound. She felt around in the dark until she found the bedside table and lantern. Finding a box of lucifers, she struck one, then held the flame to the wick as she turned up the fuel. A golden bubble of light pushed away the darkness.

Because of the wound, Gid was in a much deeper sleep than normal. He neither heard Suzy when she came into his room nor did he awaken when she lit the lantern. It was only when she sat on the bed beside him that his eyes snapped open. Even then he awoke more from curiosity than from a sense of danger.

"What?" Gid asked. "What are you doing?"

"Shh," Suzy whispered, holding her finger across her lips. She began unwinding the sheet from around his side. "I'm going to treat your wound," she said.

"It'll be all right."

"No. It must be cleaned and treated," Suzy insisted. "I have bandages and medicines."

"All right," Gid said with a sigh. "I never argue with a beautiful woman who is treating me well." He lay back on the bed.

Suzy had the sheet completely unwound now, and she sucked in her breath as she looked at the blood which had coagulated around the wound.

"You've lost a great deal of blood," she said. "You're lucky you aren't dead. Who did you make mad?"

Gid chuckled. "I don't have the slightest idea. Oh, it hurts when I laugh." He laughed again.

"Be still now," Suzy said as she poured water from the porcelain pitcher into the basin. "I'll clean your wound, then dress it."

She examined the wounds more closely. "You're lucky, it looks like the bullet was so far to the side that it didn't hit anything vital."

Gid lay back down and folded his hands behind his head. The muscles in his arms, shoulders, and chest rippled as he did so, and he looked up at the beautiful young woman who brought the water to the small table and sat again on the bed beside him.

"All right, I'll be still," he promised.

Gently, Suzy began cleaning the blood from Gid's side.

When his entry and exit wounds were completely clean, she applied a salve to them, then rubbed on the crushed medicinal herbs. "Does it feel good?" she asked.

"Yeah," Gid croaked, "as good as I can feel with two bullet holes in me."

"One bullet, two holes," Suzy said, "not to be picky."

Chapter Eleven

On Thursday morning, June twentieth, a tall, skinny, scarecrow of a man came into the jailhouse. He was carrying two coils of rope and a can of beeswax. He put the rope and can on the corner of what had been Sheriff Townsend's desk, then looked back toward the jail cell.

"Is that fella there my customer?" he asked Lewis.

"Yes, sir, Mr. Lighthouse, that's him, all right," Lewis replied. "His name is Will Crockett."

Lighthouse walked up to the jail cell and looked over at Will, who was lying on the bunk with his hands folded behind his head.

"Mr. Crockett, my name is Abner Lighthouse. It's going to be my privilege to be your hangman. Yes, sir, I'll be tellin' my grandchildren that I was the one that hung Will Crockett. Now, get up, boy. Get up an' let me take a look at you."

Will did no more than glance over at him. He made no effort to get out of his bunk.

"I said, get up," Lighthouse repeated.

Will remained motionless.

"Well, you can suit yourself," Lighthouse said. He took out a small pad and a pencil. "It ain't really goin' to change nothin', 'cause I can get quite a bit of information just by lookin' at you there. 'Course, it's to your advantage that I get it all right. If I make a mistake you could either wind up chokin', real slow...or else havin' your head pinched right off whenever you drop through the trap."

"Aren't you jumping the gun a little there, Mr. Lighthouse?" John Woodward asked, coming into the office just as Lighthouse was making his last comment.

"What do you mean?" Lighthouse asked.

"You're talking about hanging a man who hasn't been found guilty. In fact, my client hasn't even been tried."

Lighthouse laughed. "He's your client? And you're telling me he hasn't been found guilty yet?" he asked. "That's a good one." Lighthouse chewed on the end of the pencil with his teeth, exposing a little more of the pencil lead. "Now, let's see...I'd make you about five feet ten, maybe five-eleven."

Will offered no response as Lighthouse wrote the numbers in his book.

"And, I'd say, a hundred seventy, maybe a hundred

seventy-five pounds. Of course, that's before you're served your last meal," he added. "Some folks eat so much at their last meal they mess up all my cipherin'." He laughed at his joke.

"You don't have to be worryin' none about this fella eatin' too much," Lewis called over from his desk. "All I've give him to eat so far is biscuits 'n water."

Woodward looked back toward Lewis with a frown on his face. "Is that right? You've given this man nothing but biscuits and water?"

"Yeah. The way I look at it, why waste money on him? I mean, if we're only goin' to hang him, anyway."

"Is that what the judge ordered?"

"Judge don't have nothin' to do with feedin' my prisoners. I do," Lewis said.

Woodward looked at Will. "Why didn't you tell me about this?" he asked.

"I didn't figure I was going to starve in three days," Gid said. "And I figured you had enough on your mind without worrying about whether or not I was getting anything to eat."

"Get this man a meal," Woodward ordered.

Lewis bristled. "Look here, you ain't nothin' but a lawyer...and a drunken one at that. You got no say-so whatever, on how I treat my prisoners."

"I said get this man a meal," Woodward demanded.

"Or I will take this to the judge and you'll be looking for another job...that is you'll be looking for another job as soon as you get out of jail."

"Jail? What do you mean, jail? Why would I be goin' to jail?"

"Mistreatment of your prisoners is a jailable offense," Woodward said. He smiled. "In fact, I might even be able to arrange for you and Mr. Crockett to share the same cell."

"All right, all right, I'll go down to Ma Feeler's place an' get 'im some bacon and beans," Lewis said, grumbling. He slammed the door behind him as he left the office.

"What are you trying to do, John?" Lighthouse asked as he continued to make entries in his small notepad. "Cheat me out of my hangin' fee? If you get this fella off, I don't get paid."

"I intend to get him off if I can," Woodward said.

"I thought you gave up the lawyering business."

"No, I, uh, turned my back on it for a while. But I didn't give it up."

"Is that a fact? Well, tell me, John, how long have you been sober?"

"Twenty-six hours and," Woodward looked up at the clock, "fourteen minutes," he concluded.

"That long? Well, I'm just real proud of you, John. Are you having a hard time with it? I'll bet you'd like a drink now, wouldn't you?" Lighthouse started yanking open the drawers on Lewis's desk until he found what he was looking for. He held up a bottle of whiskey and read the label. "Old Overholt," he said. "Well, now, that's not exactly the brand they serve in the finest establishments, is it?" He looked over at Woodward. "But then, you haven't been all that choosy of late, have you?"

Woodward rubbed the back of his hand across his mouth. "I...I don't want that," he said.

"Oh, sure you do," Lighthouse replied in an oily-smooth voice. He found a glass that was half full of water, tossed the water out on the floor, then poured in about two fingers of whiskey. He looked at it, then shook his head. "Nah...that's not enough. Not for someone who has been dry for as long as you have." He poured the glass nearly full, then held it out toward Woodward. "Here you go," he said.

Woodward stood absolutely motionless for a long moment, staring at the glass. Will, who had not yet risen from the bunk, watched the drama being played out before him, but he offered no comment.

"I...I said I don't want it," Woodward stammered.

"Yes, I heard what you said. Tell you what I'm going to do. I'm just going to set this glass over here, on the corner of the desk. That way, if you really don't want it, why, it's over here out of harm's way, so to speak. On the other hand, if you need just a small drink to get you through all this...and, believe me, that is perfectly understandable... well, it'll be right here for you."

Chuckling, Lighthouse picked up one coil of rope, then uncoiled it. He sat down in the empty chair behind what had been Townsend's desk, and started applying beeswax to the rope. "Yes, sir," Lighthouse said. "I'll just leave that glass over there while I grease up the rope, make it slide real easy. We want the knot to break his neck. Like this." He made a circle with his thumb and forefinger, then slipped it down the rope as if it were the knot sliding. When he reached the end, he made a clucking sound, then tilted his head abruptly as if the neck had just been broken. "Otherwise, ole' Crockett there would just sort of dangle at the end of the rope, chokin' to death, real slow."

"One drink," Woodward suddenly said, starting toward the glass. He had been staring at it, ever since Lighthouse put it on the desk. "One drink won't hurt me. I need it. I can't think without it."

Fifteen minutes later, Lewis returned with Will's food. He took it over to him.

"Here," he said. "And I recommend that you enjoy it. This time tomorrow, you'll be eating supper in hell. What do you think about that?"

"I think the company in hell will be an improvement

over what I've seen in Watson," Will replied. He took the tin plate, then returned to his bunk. Sitting on the edge of his bunk, he ate the food ravenously.

Lewis looked around the office, surprised to see that no one was there.

"What happened to John and the hangman?"

"They had business elsewhere," Will replied, not looking up from his plate of beans.

A short time later the front door was pushed open and the woman Will knew only as Nora, came in. "He's been drinking again," she wailed.

"Who? You mean Woodward?" Lewis replied.

"You know full well who I mean," Nora said. "You gave him whiskey. Why? Why did you do that? Were you afraid he'd prove himself in court tomorrow?"

"Wait a minute now. You just hold on there, Missy," Lewis said, holding his hands out in front of him. "I didn't do no such thing. Last time I seen him, he was sober as a judge. Fact is, he made me go get somethin' for the prisoner to eat. Where's he at, anyhow?"

"I took him up to his room, half-drunk," Nora said. "He says he started drinking over here."

"The hell he did. I told you, last time I seen him, he was sober."

"Is that true, Mr. Crockett?" Nora asked.

"What the hell? You goin' to take a murderer's word

over mine?" Lewis asked.

"The deputy is right," Will said.

Surprised at being vindicated by Will, the deputy looked toward his cell. "'Course, on the other hand, I reckon it's all right to take his word for it when he's tellin' the truth."

"Are you telling me he wasn't drinking over here?"

"No, I'm not telling you that," Will said. "I'm just saying that the deputy had nothing to do with it. The hangman searched around until he found a bottle. That was all it took."

"Ohh," Nora groaned. She went over and sat in the chair behind Townsend's empty desk, then hung her head. "I thought...that is, I hoped...things would be better now."

Chapter Twelve

Gid heard a drum pounding and he wondered who would have a drum here and why they would be beating it. Then he awakened and realized that it wasn't a drum, it was someone banging on the door to his room.

"Crockett! Crockett, are you in there?"

Slowly, wincing at the pain in his side, Gid sat up.

"Crockett!"

Gid slipped his pistol from the holster then moved painfully over to the door.

On the other side of the door the pounding grew more desperate.

"Crockett, this is Sheriff Baxter. If you are in there, answer me!" the voice called from the other side of the door.

Without saying a word, Gid jerked the door open. That left him standing there with the drop on the sheriff, who had just raised his hand to knock again.

"What do you want?" Gid asked.

The sheriff smiled, self-consciously. "Well, I reckon you just answered that for me," he said.

"What do you mean?"

"I understand you were shot last night. I just wanted to see if you were still alive."

"I'm still alive," Gid said. "Are you disappointed?"

"Disappointed? No, not at all. I hate it when someone in my town gets killed, unless I'm the one doin' the killin'. It just causes more work for me," Baxter said.

"Yeah, well, I'm glad I didn't cause you any more work," Gid said.

"Do you need tendin' to?"

"I've been tended to."

The sheriff looked at the clean, neat bandage on Gid's side.

"I see," he said. "Looks like whoever did it, did a pretty good job."

"I've got no complaints," Gid said. "And I particularly liked the bedside manner."

Sheriff Baxter looked at Gid with a confused expression on his face, then he shook his head. "I'm not even going to ask about that," he said. "Seems to me like you and your brother have made some pretty powerful enemies."

Gid perked up. "Have you heard from my brother? Do

you know where he is?"

Sheriff Baxter shook his head no. "Sorry, I don't have any idea where he's at. Last thing he told me was he was goin' over to Gold Hill to meet you."

"Yes, that's the last thing he told me, too. Wait a minute, what do you mean, my brother and I have made some pretty powerful enemies?"

"The two men your brother killed? They started the fracas by trying to kill Will. Now, you come to town, you're here less than one day, and from what I hear you didn't rile anyone in particular. Yet, last night, someone shot you. Why?"

"I don't know."

"They are after you and your brother, but you don't know why?"

"No."

"Too bad. I was hoping you might be able to shed a little light on what's going on around here. What are your plans now?"

"Now?" Gid replied. "I plan to eat breakfast."

Fifteen minutes later, Gid and Sheriff Baxter were having breakfast together.

"Did you know my brother? Did you meet him before he had the run in with Washburn and Dixon?" Gid asked.

"Oh, yes, I met him. He came in on the train about a

week ago. He hung out over at The Desert Strike Saloon... mostly playing cards, sometimes keeping company with that woman who got herself killed."

"You are talking about Lurleen Simpson."

"Yes," Baxter said.

"Do you think there could be any connection between Lurleen getting killed and people who are trying to kill my brother and me?"

Baxter stroked his chin for a moment as he pondered the question. Finally, he shook his head. "No, I don't see how there could be," he said. "I'm pretty sure whoever killed that girl killed her for that watch she was always wearin'. 'Course, that means her killer has long since left these parts. He couldn't very well sell that watch to anyone around here, since ever'one knows that it belonged to the Simpson woman."

"Maybe one of Lurleen's customers was jealous of Will," Gid suggested. "Maybe the same person who tried to kill Will is the one who killed Lurleen."

Sheriff Baxter shook his head. "No, I don't think so. From what your brother said, someone hired Dixon and Washburn to try and kill him. Normally, people who kill out of jealousy, do it themselves."

"Yeah, I guess that's right. I'm just trying to find a reason for all this, that's all. You said Will played a lot of cards. Did he win big?"

"You mean did a sore loser hire Washburn and Dixon to kill him?" Baxter asked.

Gid nodded.

"It doesn't seem likely. Your brother had one pretty good night at cards, but from what I've heard, the other nights were pretty even. And the last night he was here, he even lost a few dollars. At any rate, there wasn't enough money changed hands in any given game to cause anyone to be all that upset. Besides which, the fellas he played cards with are all upstanding citizens. I'm sure none of them had anything to do with it."

"Then what is it? Why did someone try to kill him?"

"You tell me, Mr. Crockett. Whatever it is, it's pretty obvious the trouble didn't start here."

"You say that, Sheriff, but Will was attacked here, and so was I. Nothing happened to me while I was in Gold Hill."

"Listen, are you sure your brother didn't make it to Gold Hill? Maybe he did, and you just missed him over there."

"I know he didn't make it. Because when he didn't show up, I started backtracking, and I found his horse out on the trail."

"What happened to the horse?"

"Someone shot it."

"Maybe Will shot it his ownself. Maybe his horse

stepped in a hole or something and Will—"

"No," Joe interrupted. "There was nothing wrong with the horse except for the bullet hole in his neck. It was a rifle bullet. A 44-40."

"Did you look around?"

"I looked, but I couldn't track him, because a sandstorm took out all the tracks. I figured he either had to go on through to Gold Hill or come back here to Thornburg."

"Well, I'm absolutely positive he didn't come back here," Baxter said. "We're a small enough town, and Will made himself well enough known in that shoot-out that, if he had come back, I would know it."

"He didn't go to Gold Hill, either," Gid said. "And I'm sure he didn't wander off into the desert. He's much too smart for something like that. And I know he didn't disappear into thin air."

"Maybe he went to Watson," Sheriff Baxter suggested.

Gid looked up from his breakfast in surprise. "Watson? Where is Watson? I've never heard of it."

"It's about half way on a line between here and Gold Hill, though maybe twenty miles to the south. The three towns make a triangle in Open Valley."

"Are you sure there is such a place?" Gid asked. "I didn't see it on the map."

"Of course it's on the map. It's...wait a minute, what map are you talking about? Let me see it. Do you have it with you?"

"No. But there was a map on the wall of the bank over in Gold Hill. I checked it over pretty good before I came here."

Sheriff Baxter grinned. "The McGruder Map. I should've thought of that."

"The McGruder Map?"

"McGruder is an engraver from San Francisco. He does maps for such places as banks, saloons, railroad depots and the like. They're for show. They aren't meant to be used for anything more than that. Didn't you notice all the art work? The mountain lions, the lizards, cactus, old, abandoned mines, and the like? He even draws little trains on the tracks between the towns. Only, sometimes, if something gets in the way of one of his pictures—a town for instance—why he'll just leave the town out. On the latest map he drew, he left out the town of Watson. Instead, he drew a picture of a cloud, complete with a face and pursed lips blowing wind. The thing is, those maps are everywhere, and lots of people take them for real."

"Yeah, like I did," Gid said disgustedly. "Watson, huh? Thanks, Sheriff, you've been a big help." He left a coin on the table beside his plate, then he stood up.

"Where are you going?" Baxter asked.

"I'm going to Watson. Will has to be there."

"That's a pretty long ride," Baxter said. "There's an

111

easier way to find out than by going there."

"How's that?"

"Simple. I'll wire the sheriff and ask him if he's seen Will.""You know the sheriff over there?"

"Yeah," Baxter said. "I know him. I don't like the son of a bitch, but I know him. He's always been a particular favorite of the district judge, Judge Huff. With any other judge, Townsend would have probably been jailed a long time ago for being too quick with his gun."

"Can you trust him?"

"I wouldn't trust him any farther than I could throw him if he had any personal stake in the matter," Baxter admitted. "But as far as just providing information on whether or not your brother might be in Watson, well, I can't think of any reason why Townsend would lie about it. Come on, we'll send a telegram over there and see if they've heard anything."

Gid walked down to the Western Union office with Sheriff Baxter, then stood by as Baxter wrote out the message. He handed the message across the open counter to the telegrapher.

"Get this over to Sheriff Townsend in Watson," Baxter said. "And ask for an immediate reply. We'll wait right here for it."

"Oh, my, you still haven't found your brother, Mr. Crockett?" the telegrapher asked. "Well, I'll get this right out and see if we can get some word for you."

"Thanks," Gid said.

Gid leaned up against the wall with his arms folded across his chest as he watched the telegrapher's fingers operate the key. There were several clacks going out, then, a moment later, the key began clacking on its own. Gid realized that this was an incoming message from the other end, and he walked over to be there when the message ended. It wasn't a very long message.

"Odd," the telegrapher said.

"What's odd?"

"The message just says, 'unable to deliver.'"

"They don't tell you why?"

"No, sir."

"Raise 'em again. Find out why,"

Again the key clacked with both the outgoing message, and the incoming. With a face devoid of all expression, the telegrapher wrote out the message as it came in, then he handed it to Baxter. He glanced, once at Gid, as Baxter read the message.

"What is it, sheriff?" Gid asked. "What does the message say?"

"Sheriff Townsend's dead," Baxter said. "He's been murdered."

"Murdered?"

"That's what it says here."

"Damn. So we still don't know if Will is there."

"Oh, he's there, all right," Baxter said.

"What? He's there? How do you know?"

Without a word, Baxter handed the telegram to Gid.

SHERIFF TOWNSEND MURDERED BY ITINER-ANT NAMED WILL CROCKETT. TRIAL AND EXE-CUTION SET FOR TOMORROW.

"Trial and execution?" Gid said after reading the telegram.

"With the judge they've got over there, justice is rarely honest or fair, but it is quick," Sheriff Baxter said. "If you want to see your brother alive again, I'd suggest that you get yourself up to Watson as soon as you can."

"Thank you, Sheriff, I intend to."

Chapter Thirteen

"Oyez, oyez, oyez, this court is now in session, draw near all who have business with this court, the honorable Judge Mason Huff, presiding. All rise."

Huff, wearing a robe, came into the courtroom and took his seat. Amidst the sound of scraping chairs and the rustle of pants and dress fabric, the gallery also sat. A spittoon rang with the quid of a well-aimed expectoration.

Court was being held in the town's all-purpose community room, which was utilized for everything from town meetings, to dances, to church revivals, to its current use as a courtroom. Though not designed specifically as a courtroom, it was far superior to some of the other places that were put to that use in small, western communities, such as schoolrooms or even saloons.

Huff stared out over his desk at the two tables that had been placed in front of the room, one for the prosecutor and one for the defense. At the prosecutor's table he saw Oscar Haydon busily arranging his notes. At the defense table Will Crockett was sitting alone.

"Did you dismiss your counsel, Mr. Crockett?" Judge Huff asked.

"No."

"Where is he?"

"I don't know. I haven't seen him this morning," Will replied.

Huff glared at Lewis. "Mr. Lewis, I deem it your responsibility to have counsel present when trial begins. Counsel is not present; therefore, I am fining you five dollars."

"Judge, that ain't fair," Lewis protested. "Like as not, the son of a bitch is off drunk some 'eres. I don't know why I should be held to blame."

"Make that fine ten dollars, Mr. Lewis," Judge Huff said. "Do you care to go on?"

"No, Your Honor," Lewis said contritely.

"I didn't think so. Now, please go find him, and bring him here."

"Yes, Your Honor," Lewis said.

Huff turned toward the prosecutor's table. "Mr. Haydon, you may present your opening comments."

"Wait!" a female voice called, rushing in through the back door, just as Lewis was leaving. There was a buzz of surprise from this unexpected interruption, and Huff looked up with an obvious expression of irritation on his face.

"Who called out?" Huff asked.

"I did, Your Honor."

When Will turned to see who it was, he saw that it was Nora, the same young woman he had met, the day before.

"And you are?"

"You know who I am, Your Honor."

"Yes, Miss Woodward, I know who you are. But I want you to state it for the court record," Huff said, patronizingly.

"I am Nora Woodward, daughter of the defense counsel."

That was a surprise to Will, but what came next was an even bigger surprise.

"And co-counsel for the defense," she added.

"You are co-counsel?"

"Yes, Your Honor."

Judge Woodward stroked his chin. "I knew that you had been reading the law with your father," he said. "But I wasn't aware that you had passed the bar."

"I haven't passed the bar, Your Honor. But according to the New Mexico Code, if I have the defendant's acquiescence, and your permission, I can act as co-counsel."

"I see," Judge Huff said. He looked over at Will. "Tell

117

me, Mr. Crockett. Do you give this girl permission to act as your co-counsel?"

"Why not?" Will replied. "At least she is sober."

The courtroom erupted into laughter, but Huff's gavel quieted them.

"I'll have none of that in my court," he said. He addressed Nora. "Girl, where is your father?"

"He'll be here shortly," Nora replied. "He was unavoidably detained."

"Unavoidably detained," Huff repeated.

"Yes, Your Honor."

Huff looked at Nora for a long time then, finally, nodded his head. "Very well, Miss Woodward, you may act as co-counsel."

"Thank you, Your Honor. And I have an immediate objection."

"You have an objection? What could you possibly be objecting? The trial hasn't even started."

"Yes, sir, it has," Nora insisted, speaking, even as she was walking up to take her position at the defendant's table. "As I was entering the courtroom, I heard you invite Mr. Haydon to present his opening comments. But there has been no voir dire."

"Mr. Haydon and I have already taken care of that," Huff said. "We questioned the jurors quite thoroughly this morning, and found them acceptable. I acted on your father's behalf, since he wasn't present."

"But surely you can't—"

"Your objection is overruled, Miss Woodward, if defense counsel had wanted to be present for voir dire, one of you had every opportunity to do so. Since neither of you showed up, I took the responsibility of conducting voir dire for you. Now, Mr. Haydon, you may present your opening remarks," Huff said.

"Thank you, Your Honor," Haydon said. He stood up and looked over toward the jury. "Gentlemen of the jury, today you are going to be asked to undertake an awesome responsibility. You are going to be asked, not only to pass judgment on a fellow human being, but to sanction the taking of that man's life on this very day, by way of hanging.

"However, when I present all the facts in this case, the defendant's callous disregard for the code by which we all live, as well as the eyewitnesses to this cold-blooded murder, then you will have no personal difficulty in bringing forth a verdict of guilty and assessing the punishment as death." Haydon paused for a moment, then looked over toward Will before his dramatic conclusion. "Death by hanging," he said.

"Defense?"

"What?" Nora asked, looking up as if distracted.

"Do you have any opening comments, Miss Woodward?"

"Uh, no Your Honor. Defense has no opening comments."

"Very well. Prosecution, you may proceed with your case."

"Are you just going to sit there and say nothing?" Will whispered.

"I've never tried a case before," Nora replied. "But I know that sometimes it's better to say nothing, than to say the wrong thing. I'd rather leave all that to my father."

"Yes, your father. Where is he?"

"He, uh, had a difficult time last night. It is taking him a while to pull himself together this morning."

"You mean he is hung over," Will said.

"He is making an effort, Mr. Crockett. If only you knew what an effort he is making. He will be here. He promised me he would, and I believe him."

"I admire your loyalty, Miss Woodward, but the truth is, I'm probably better off with him absent."

"No, you're not. My father is a good lawyer. I will admit that he has fallen on some bad times, but he is a good lawyer."

Haydon stood then, to call his first witness.

"Your Honor, although I have depositions from half a dozen who were present when Sheriff Townsend was shot, I am only going to call Ben Lanagan. I do that because all of their testimony is virtually the same. Should defense counsel wish to question any of the others, prosecution has no objections."

"Call your witness, Counselor," Huff said.

"Prosecution calls Mr. Ben Lanagan."

Ben Lanagan was a man of average height and weight. He was about thirty-five, though a lifetime of hard work made him look older. He raised his right hand to be sworn.

"You swear to tell the truth, the whole truth, and nothing but the truth, so help you God?" the clerk asked.

Lanagan spit a wad of tobacco into the spittoon, then wiped his mouth with the back of his hand before he answered.

"I do."

During the questioning that followed, Lanagan told how he had been standing at the end of the bar nearest the door. He heard a shot from outside, and, turning, saw Townsend staggering, back-pedaling through the bat-wing doors. He fell on a table, by his weight and the force of his fall, broke it into two pieces, then wound up on his back, on the floor.

"Did Sheriff Townsend say anything?" Haydon asked.

"No, he was deader'n shit by the time he hit the floor," Lanagan said.

There was a tittering of laughter from the gallery.

"You say you heard a shot from outside. How many shots did you hear?"

"One."

"Only one shot?"

"That's all."

"Is it possible that there were two shots, but fired almost simultaneously, thus giving the illusion of one shot?" Haydon asked.

"I don't know how that could be."

"Why is that?"

"Townsend didn't even have his gun out. It was still in the holster when he hit the floor."

"Thank you, Mr. Lanagan. I have no further questions."

"Miss Woodward?" Huff asked.

As Nora approached the witness, Lanagan turned toward the judge.

"Judge, are you goin' to let this here girl ask me questions like she was a lawyer?"

"As far as you are concerned, Mr. Lanagan, she is a lawyer," Huff replied. "And you will answer accordingly."

"Yes, sir. Well, I'll say this. I ain't never seen me no prettier lawyer anywheres," Lanagan said. Again the gallery laughed, and they were quieted this time only by a warning glare from Judge Huff.

"Mr. Lanagan," Nora began. "Did you hear any exchange of words between Sheriff Townsend and Mr.

Crockett?"

"Naw. It was too noisy inside the saloon. First thing I heard was the shot."

"And you saw nothing?"

"Yeah, I saw something. I seen Townsend come backin' through the doors."

"But, of the actual shooting, you saw nothing?"

"No, that happened out front, on the porch."

"Then you cannot testify as to who drew first, can you?"

"Girly, I didn't have to see it to know who drawed first. I tole' you, the gun was still in Townsend's holster."

"Isn't it possible that Mr. Crockett saw Townsend starting for his gun, but drew his own gun so quickly that Townsend was stopped before he could draw?" Nora asked.

Lanagan looked at Nora in total surprise. "Are you tryin' to say this here Crockett fella is so fast that he could draw and shoot before Townsend could even clear leather?" He laughed. "That's the most damn fool notion I've ever heard," he said. The gallery laughed with him.

"No further questions, Your Honor," Nora said, her cheeks flaming as she returned to the defense table.

"Redirect, Mr. Haydon?"

"No redirect," Haydon replied. "Your Honor, despite the obvious inexperience of the defense counsel, I would like to point out that she did bring up one salient point. Neither Mr. Lanagan, nor anyone else in the saloon, actually witnessed the shooting. But there is one person who did see the shooting, and that will be my final witness. Prosecution calls to the stand the widow, Mrs. May Scanlon."

May Scanlon was a dried up, pinch-faced, perch-mouthed woman. Her hair was combed back into a severe bun, and a pair of rimless glasses rested on the end of her nose. After being sworn, she took her seat in the witness chair. As she waited for the cross-examination to begin, she fidgeted with the dark gray, high-collar dress she was wearing.

Haydon got up from his table, and hooking his thumbs in his vest, approached the witness chair. He smiled and nodded, deferentially.

"Now, Mrs. Scanlon, I realize that it is a difficult thing to testify in a case like this, and I want you to know how much I appreciate your agreeing to do so."

"I'm only doing my Christian duty," Mrs. Scanlon replied self-righteously.

"To be sure," Haydon replied. "Now, on the night Sheriff Townsend was murdered..."

"Objection, Your Honor," Nora interrupted. "It has not been established that Sheriff Townsend was murdered, only that he was killed."

"Sustained," Huff said.

"Very good, Miss Woodward," Haydon said. Looking at her, he clapped his hands slowly, and patronizingly. "I'm sure your father, if he were here... and sober, would be pleased with you. And you are quite correct, my comment was prejudicial. Therefore, I will rephrase my question." He turned back to the witness. "Now, Mrs. Scanlon, on the night Sheriff Townsend was," he paused and looked over toward Nora as he said the next word, setting it apart from the rest of his sentence, "...killed...were you in your apartment?"

"I was."

"And, what night was that?"

"That would have been Tuesday night, the eighteenth, instant," Mrs. Scanlon replied.

"Let the record show that Mrs. Scanlon has established the date on which Sheriff Townsend was killed as Tuesday, June the eighteenth," Haydon said.

"So ordered," Huff said.

Haydon turned back to Mrs. Scanlon. "How far is your apartment from the front porch of The Whistle Stop Saloon?"

"Not very far at all," Mrs. Scanlon answered. "My business establishment is just next door to The Whistle Stop. Before my husband died, he was half owner of The Whistle Stop. After he died, I sold my husband's interest to Mr. Baker, the current owner of The Whistle Stop, and I used the money to buy the dress-making and alteration shop I now run."

"Would you say you are close enough to the entrance to be able to hear a conversation that might have taken place on the front porch?"

"Yes, when the window is raised in my apartment, I can easily hear conversations from the front porch of the saloon. In fact, I have overheard some quite shocking things."

"I'll say. You've gotten more than one husband in trouble with that wagging tongue of yours," someone in the gallery shouted and all laughed. With a stern glare and pounding gavel, Huff restored order.

"On the night of the eighteenth, Mrs. Scanlon, did you have cause to raise the window?"

"Yes. As you may recall, it was quite warm that evening," Mrs. Scanlon replied.

"Did you hear anything of interest on that night?"

"I heard Sheriff Townsend and another man talking."

"The other man that you overheard, is he now in court?"

"Yes."

"Can you point him out for the court?"

Mrs. Scanlon looked over toward the defense table at Will. Then she pointed at him. "That is the man."

"Thank you, Mrs. Scanlon. Your Honor, let the record show that Mrs. Scanlon has identified the defendant, Will Crockett, as the man she overheard having a conversation with Sheriff Townsend."

"So ordered," Huff replied.

"Was there anything about their conversation that caused— "

"Please the Court, Your Honor, I have Mr. Woodward," Lewis suddenly shouted, interrupting the preceding as he pushed in, importantly, through the back door.

Chapter Fourteen

"Mr. Woodward, you are late," Huff said.

"I beg your pardon, Your Honor, but I was unavoidably detained."

"More'n likely, he was unavoidably hungover," someone in the courtroom said just under his breath, and the others laughed.

Huff silenced the court with his gavel, then he looked at John. "Are you intoxicated, Mr. Woodward?"

"I am not intoxicated at the moment, Your Honor," John said.

"Approach the bench, please."

John walked down to the front of the courtroom and stood there while Judge Huff looked him over.

"Let me smell your breath," Huff demanded.

"With all due respect, Your Honor, I...uh...was intoxicated last night and there may be some residual odor. I submit that smelling my breath is not a valid test."

Huff studied John for a long moment. "All right," Huff finally said. "You don't appear to be intoxicated. And due to the court's awareness of your current economic conditions, I will not fine you for contempt for being late. However, Mr. Woodward, you are put on notice. I will not tolerate any further disregard of this court. Do you understand?"

"I do, Your Honor."

Huff nodded toward the defendant's table. "You may take your seat with your client and your co-counsel," he said.

"Thank you, Your Honor."

"Prosecution may continue."

"Clerk, would you read back my last question, please?" Haydon asked.

The clerk read in a monotone voice: "Was there anything about their conversation that caused....and that is as far as you got."

"Thank you. Mrs. Scanlon, was there anything in their conversation that caused you to pay particular attention to what they were saying?"

"I don't understand the question."

"Were their words loud or angry?"

"Loud? Angry? No," Mrs. Scanlon replied, "but they were frightening."

"They weren't loud or angry, but they were frightening? How so?"

"The words were cold and calculating," Mrs. Scanlon said.

"Cold and calculating. Would you say they were killing words?"

"Objection," John called out. "Prosecution is leading the witness."

"Sustained."

"All right, I'll strike that. We'll go with cold, calculating, and frightening. Did there seem to be a disagreement between them?"

"Yes," Mrs. Scanlon said.

"And what was the disagreement about?"

"Evidently Mr. Crockett wanted to go into the saloon, but the sheriff was opposed to that."

"What makes you think that?"

"I heard the sheriff say, 'Mister, I told you, you ain't comin' in here and that's just the way it's goin' to be.'"

"How did Crockett respond?"

"He didn't say anything," Mrs. Scanlon said. "So the sheriff spoke again. 'Time's runnin' short,' the sheriff said. 'What are you goin' to do?'"

"Was there a reply to that?" Haydon asked.

"Yes. Mr. Crockett said, 'I'm going to do just what I told you I was going to do. I'm going in there to get myself some supper and a couple of beers. Now, you can either step aside and let me by, or stay where you are while I come through you.' "

Haydon turned toward the jury and held his finger up. "Step aside and let me by, or stay where you are while I come through you," he said. He turned back to Mrs. Scanlon. "What was said next?"

"Nothing was said next," Mrs. Scanlon replied.

"Nothing? You mean nothing else happened?"

Mrs. Scanlon shook her head. "I didn't say that. I said no more words were spoken. The next thing I knew, there was a gun in Mr. Crockett's hand. I saw the flash and heard the sound of the shot."

"Then what?"

"Then Mr. Crockett passed out of my view, going into the saloon."

"Now, Mrs. Scanlon, and this is very important," Haydon said. "Did you see who drew first?"

"Yes."

"And, who drew first?"

"Mr. Crockett drew first," she said. "One moment there was nothing in his hand, and the next moment...almost as quick as thought, he was holding, and shooting his gun."

"Thank you," Haydon said. He looked over at the defense table. "Your witness, Mr. Woodward."

John got up from the defense table and walked over

to Mrs. Scanlon.

"Mrs. Scanlon, did you see Sheriff Townsend start to draw?"

"No."

"You didn't see him draw, because in fact, you didn't see him at all. Is that correct?"

"Objection! It has already been established that Mrs. Scanlon was a witness through her window, that night!"

"I submit, Your Honor, that Mrs. Scanlon was a witness to only one-half of the drama. One of the reasons I was late this morning, is because I asked Mrs. Scanlon's maid to allow me into her apartment so I could examine the window through which she witnessed the shooting. In doing so, I discovered an interesting fact. From the chair Mrs. Scanlon occupies during her window eavesdrops, her view of the front of the saloon is limited. She can see the front steps to the porch, but, because of the porch roof, a significant part of the porch is blocked from her view." John then turned his attention back to the witness. "You heard them both speaking that night, but, you didn't actually see Sheriff Townsend. That's true, isn't it, Mrs. Scanlon?"

"Well, yes, if you mean did I actually see the sheriff, then the answer is no. He wasn't in my direct view."

"That being the case, it is very possible that Sheriff Townsend started his draw before Mr. Crockett, but you didn't see it."

Mrs. Scanlon shook her head. "Based on what I was seeing, and overhearing, I just don't think that is the way it happened. I stand by my statement that Mr. Crockett drew first."

"I see," John said. He started back toward his table then he stopped and looked back at her. "Mrs. Scanlon, you didn't actually see Mr. Crockett start his draw either, did you?"

"I beg your pardon?"

John closed the rest of the distance to his table, then read from his notes, "You said, and I quote, 'One moment there was nothing in his hand, and the next moment... almost as quick as thought, he was holding, and shooting his gun.' By your own account Mrs. Scanlon, Mr. Crockett was so fast, that you didn't see him start his draw. You saw only the conclusion...when the gun was actually in his hand. But a conclusion must have a beginning. He obviously started his draw, even though you didn't see it. Isn't that correct?"

"Yes...I...I suppose that is so," Mrs. Scanlon agreed.

"So then, if you didn't see either man begin their draw, it is impossible for you to say who drew first."

"I...I guess so."

"Thus, Mr. Crockett's statement that Sheriff Townsend drew first remains unchallenged by any eyewitness," John said triumphantly to the jury. He turned back toward Mrs. Scanlon, who was still sitting in the witness chair. A look of confusion had replaced what had been an expression of smug correctness.

"Thank you, Mrs. Scanlon. No further questions," John said as he sat down. Smiling in support, Nora put her hand on her father's arm.

"Redirect, Mr. Haydon?" Huff asked.

Haydon stood, but he didn't leave his table. "Mrs. Scanlon, before the incident the other night, did you ever have occasion to see Sheriff Townsend use his gun?"

"Yes, when my husband was alive and running the saloon. I was witness to a gunfight between Sheriff Townsend, R. J. Kingston, and Frank Garriga."

"Yes, I remember that. In fact, you gave testimony in court in regard to that shooting, did you not?"

"I did."

"On that occasion, by his speed and skill with a pistol, Sheriff Townsend prevailed over not one, but two would be assassins?"

"Yes."

"So, even if, as defense claims, you were unable to see Sheriff Townsend on the night of the eighteenth, you have in fact seen him in action before."

"Yes, I have."

"Now, on the night of the eighteenth, you saw Mr.

Crockett, which means you have seen both men under similar conditions. Based upon your observation, which of the two do you think is the faster?"

"Objection!" John said. "Your Honor, you can't ask a person to make a comparison based upon seeing one person draw at one time, and another at another time. She would have to see both of them at the same time!"

"Your Honor, I'm not really asking the witness to make a comparison in the sense Mr. Woodward is thinking. She has already testified that she believed Crockett drew first. I am just providing her with the empirical evidence that will allow her to substantiate the belief she has already stated."

"Defense objection is overruled," Huff said.

"Exception! To allow such convoluted logic would be a gross miscarriage of justice," John shouted.

"Be very, very careful with me, Mr. Woodward," Judge Huff warned, shaking his finger at him. "I have said I will allow Mr. Haydon's argument to stand and that's it."

"Thank you, Your Honor," Haydon said. "I have no more questions."

Chapter Fifteen

"Yes, I know Watson," Suzy said. She shuddered. "I used to live there. It was only for a short while, but that was much too long. It's a terrible town."

"What's bad about it?" Gid asked.

"They say a town is only as good as its law, and in Watson, the law is a man named Ernest Townsend. Sheriff Townsend is the evilest man I have ever known. He terrorizes the girls who are in my trade. He demands that we either provide him with free services or we wind up in jail."

"His way of saving money, I suppose."

"No," Suzy said with a grim expression. "It wasn't just the money. Girls like us often have to provide free service to men in power, it's part of the trade. But with Townsend it was more than that. He is a particularly cruel man who gets some sort of enjoyment out of causing pain. And not just physical pain, he also causes ..." Suzy paused, trying to come up with the right word.

"Emotional pain?" Gid suggested.

"Yes," Suzy said. "And in the case of Wanda Jean, the pain was too much for her. She committed suicide. That was why I left."

"Townsend won't be causing anyone else any pain," Gid said.

Suzy shook her head. "No, I'm afraid you are wrong there. Someone like Townsend won't change until the day he dies."

"Well, waiting until he dies is not a problem. Townsend is dead. My brother killed him."

"Good for your brother," Suzy said decisively.

"Maybe not so good. From what I understand, they plan to try him and hang him on the same day."

"Oh, Gid! No! What are you going to do?"

"I'm going to Watson. I don't intend to let that happen," Gid said resolutely.

"Carl Edwards," Suzy said.

"What?"

"When you get there, go see Carl Edwards. He owns the livery stable and he's a good man. Tell him Suzy Jenkins sent you, and if there is anything he can do to help, he will."

"Thanks," Gid replied.

Del Starkey climbed up onto a rock from which he could see for nearly two miles back across the desert. A small rise hid everything beyond that point.

"See anything?" Rhiny Brown asked.

"No," Starkey answered.

Brown, a short, hairy man with gray eyes and a pug nose took the last swallow from a whiskey bottle, then tossed it against a nearby rock. The bottle broke into two pieces.

"Goddammit, Brown, what for'd you break that bottle?" Starkey asked, looking around at him. "We could'a got us five cents for it back in town."

"Five cents," Brown snorted. "If you'd sell that gold tooth of your'n, you'd get a lot more than five cents."

"I ain't goin' to sell my gold tooth. If you're so all-fired anxious to sell somethin', we could sell the watch you got."

"You keep your hands off my watch. Anyhow, the deal we got goin' now is goin' to bring us more money than your gold tooth or my watch," Brown said.

"Yeah, well, I ain't seen no money yet."

"All we have to do is take care of the Crocketts, and we'll get our share," Brown insisted. "Now, look again."

"We ain't got Will Crockett to worry about now. He'll be hung before nightfall."

"Don't count your chickens before they hatch," Brown cautioned. "When you shot his horse, you thought the son of a bitch would die on the desert, but he didn't. You should'a killed him when you had the chance."

"Who would'a thought he would make as far as he did?" Starkey replied. "Anyway, the judge'll take care of him."

"That leaves Gid Crockett for us."

"Maybe he ain't comin'," Starkey said.

"He's comin'," Brown said. "I can feel it in my gut. He is out there, and he's close."

Starkey climbed down from the rock and walked over to his horse. He slipped his rifle out of the saddle holster.

"What are you fixin' to do?" Brown asked.

"If he's really comin', like you say he is, I don't aim to let him get any closer'n a rifle shot.

"Yeah," Brown agreed. "Yeah, that's a good idea. We'll just shoot the son of a bitch down, soon as he comes into range."

The two men, with rifles in hand, climbed back up onto the rock which afforded them not only a good view of the approaching trail, but also some cover and concealment. They checked the loads in their rifles, eased the hammers back to half-cock, then hunkered down on the rock and waited.

"Let 'im come up to no more'n about a hunnert yards," Brown suggested. "We got all the advantage. He don't have no idea we're here a' waitin' on 'im."

"I still say he ain't comin'," Starkey said.

At that moment, a rider came into view over a distant rise.

"He ain't, huh?" Brown said with the smug air of 'I told you so.' "Then who is that?"

"Son of a bitch! It's him!" Starkey said. He raised his rifle to his shoulder.

"Hold it!" Brown said, reaching out to pull the rifle back down. "Be patient. You shoot now, you won't do no more'n spook him. Let him get close, like I said."

"All right," Starkey said, nervously.

They waited as the distant rider came closer, sometimes seeming not to be riding, but rather floating as he materialized and dematerialized in the heat waves that were rising from the desert floor.

On he came, to a mile, half a mile, a quarter mile. Brown raised his rifle and rested it carefully against the rock, taking a very careful aim. "Just a little closer," he said, quietly. "A little closer before we fire."

Starkey shifted position to get a better aim. As he did so he dislodged a loose stone, and the stone rolled down the rock, right into the largest, unbroken piece of the whiskey bottle. The stone shattered the glass and it made a loud, tinkling noise.

"Goddammit!" Brown shouted angrily. "You dumb bastard, you just gave away our position!" He raised up and fired his first shot.

The sound of the crashing bottle reached Gid Crockett's ears at about the same time Brown reared up to fire. Gid could see that ahead, on the trail, a man was holding a rifle pointed at him.

"What the hell?" he shouted, pulling his pistol at the same time. He snapped off a shot, knowing he was out of range, hoping only to make the ambusher hurry his own shot. The ploy worked. Brown fired, then dropped back down behind the rock.

Gid slid down from his horse quickly, slipping his rifle from the holster as he did so. Slapping his horse to get him out of the line of fire, he ran, bending over, toward a nearby rock formation. Two shots whined off the rocks just as he got behind them. The shots were so close together that, even though he had only seen one man, he knew that there were at least two of them laying for him.

Gid raised up and fired his rifle toward the place where the shots had come from. Looking around, he saw a dry creek bed. If he could make it there, he could work his way up closer to the ambushers without coming under their fire.

Starkey, you dumb son of a bitch!" Brown swore. "Iffen you hadn't kicked that rock down we would'a had him by now."

"Hell, I'm not the one put the bottle there," Starkey said. "Where is he, anyhow?" Starkey stuck his head cautiously over the rock and looked down where the target had been. "Where is he? I can't see him."

"I don't know," Brown admitted. "I saw him get behind that rock, but I ain't seen him since."

"There's a dry creek bed down there. I seen it when we come through," Starkey said.

Brown looked toward him. "A dry creek bed? Damn, he could be right on us before we even knew it."

Starkey shook his head. "I don't think so," he said. "It curves away a long time before it gets up here."

No sooner were the words out of Starkey's mouth than there was a puff of smoke and the bark of a rifle from a clump of bushes not too far distant. The bullet hit the rock right in front of them, then hummed off, but not before shaving off a sliver of lead to kick up into Starkey's face.

"Ow! I been hit, I been hit!" Starkey called, slapping his hand to his face. "I been shot right in the jaw!"

Brown looked at him, then laughed.

"What do you think is so goddammed funny?" Starkey complained.

"You are. You are funny," Brown said. "You ain't been hit. That ain't nothin' but a shaving."

Two more bullets hit the rocks then and chips of stone flew past them.

"I don't like this," Brown said. "He's gettin' too damn close." Brown fired a couple of shots toward the bush just below the puff of gun smoke.

"Hey, Brown, look down there," Starkey said. "Ain't that his horse comin' back up the road?"

"Yeah," Brown said. He giggled. "This is great! Shoot the horse! We'll just leave the son of a bitch out here to die."

"That didn't work the other time. What makes you think it'll work this time?" Starkey asked.

"Do you have a better idea?" Brown challenged.

"No," Starkey admitted.

"Then shoot the goddamned horse."

Both men started shooting at the horse, but the animal was still a couple of hundred yards away and slightly downhill. As a result, it wasn't hit, though the bullets striking the ground nearby caused the horse to turn and run toward the shelter of a bluff, a quarter of a mile away.

"Dammit! We missed!" Brown said.

Another bullet hit the rock, very close beside them.

"Let's get the hell out of here!" Starkey shouted. He started running for his own horse.

"Starkey! Come back here!" Brown called, chasing after him.

Seeing the two men start to run, Gid tracked them with his rifle, firing at the man in the lead. That man went down, but the other made it to his horse. He kicked his horse into motion and in just a few seconds was behind a rocky ledge, out of the line of fire.

"Don't leave me, you bastard!" the one on the ground shouted. "Don't you leave me!"

Gid approached the man on the ground, holding his weapon pointed toward him. Seeing him, the man sat up and threw up his hands. "Don't shoot, don't shoot," he begged. "I'm hurt. I'm hurt bad."

"Your name is Starkey?" Gid asked, when he reached the wounded man.

Starkey looked surprised. How do you know my name?"

"You two boys weren't exactly keepin' secrets," Gid said. "I heard the other man call your name. Why did you ambush me?"

"You got to get me to the doctor," Starkey said, without answering Gid's question. "If this wound ain't treated, I could wind up losin' my leg."

"That's right, you could," Gid said laconically. Putting his rifle down, he knelt beside Starkey. He cut the trouser leg away with his knife and saw the ugly black hole where the rifle bullet had gone into the flesh. The bullet had come out the other side. There was a goodly amount of blood, but it wasn't pumping as it would have been had an artery been hit. And there didn't appear to be any shattered bone. Gid ripped up some more of Starkey's trouser leg and used it to make a bandage, tying it in place with strips of cloth.

"You aren't hurt all that bad," he said.

"The hell I ain't. What do you know about it, anyway?"

"I've treated gunshot wounds before."

"Yeah, well, you ain't ever treated one of mine."

"The one who got away," Gid said. "What was his name?"

"Why the hell should I tell you that?"

Gid pulled his gun and put the barrel of his pistol to Starkey's forehead.

"Because I'll shoot you if you don't."

"You're bluffing."

Gid cocked his pistol. "When you get to hell, say hello to Quantrill for me," he said, matter-of-factly. His finger twitched on the trigger.

"No, wait!" Starkey screamed as he pissed in his pants. "His name is Brown. Rhiny Brown!"

Gid eased the hammer down on his pistol. "Now, Starkey, why are you and Rhiny Brown trying to kill me?"

"Why does anyone do anything? For money," Starkey explained. He was still shaking with fear.

"Money? Where are you going to get money from killing me? There's no paper out on me out here. How do you expect to collect a reward?" Gid asked.

"A reward? Who's looking for a reward?" Starkey asked.

Gid was confused. "You said you were trying to kill me for money. If there's no reward, where's the money coming from?"

"Are you kidding?" Starkey replied. "Hell, you should know better'n anyone, where the money is coming from."

Gid had no idea what Starkey was talking about, but he decided to let it drop for the moment. Instead, he went over to Starkey's horse and started to mount.

"Hey, wait a minute! What are you doin'? You're stealin' my horse," Starkey said.

"I'm just borrowing it to ride down to collect mine," Gid said. "I'll be back in a minute or two."

"How do I know you'll be back? You could be lyin', plannin' to leave me out here."

"I could be," Gid said, easily.

Gid rode down to where his own horse stood, quietly waiting. He got off Starkey's horse and mounted his own, then returned, leading the animal he had borrowed.

"You come back. I didn't figure you'd come back," Starkey said.

"Get on," Gid ordered. "We're going into Watson."

Starkey mounted with some effort, though Gid was of the opinion that Starkey was letting on as if he was hurting much more than he was.

Gid's opinion was right. Starkey was playing for time, looking for the right moment. When Gid turned away from him, Starkey figured that the right moment had arrived. He pulled a hidden pistol from his bedroll and fired at Gid.

Until that moment, Starkey's plan had gone well. He had caught Gid by surprise, pulling and firing his pistol before Gid even realized that a second gun existed. But he missed, and that was his error. His fatal error, as it turned out, because even as Starkey's bullet was whizzing by Gid's head, Gid was already turning, his pistol blazing in his hand.

Gid's bullet caught Starkey in the chest, knocking him from his horse and killing him before he even hit the ground.

Gid rode over to Starkey's body and looked down at it. He gave a passing thought to burying him, then shrugged. Let the buzzards have the bastard.

Chapter Sixteen

"A demonstration?" Huff asked. "What sort of demonstration?"

"A demonstration of my client's expertise with the pistol, Your Honor," John said.

"Let me see if I understand this. You are asking me to put a weapon in the hand of your client...put a gun in the hand of a known killer, so he can give us a demonstration of his skills with that instrument?"

"Yes, Your Honor," John replied.

"What makes you think I would even consider such a ridiculous request?"

"Because, Your Honor, my entire case depends upon it," John said. "Prosecution claims that Mr. Crockett drew first. He had to draw first, prosecution argues, because no man alive is fast enough to have beaten Sheriff Townsend. But it is our contention that Mr. Crockett is fast enough to have done that very thing."

"Your Honor, what would a demonstration accomplish?" Haydon asked. "If the court watches him pull a pistol from his holster, we might all agree that he is fast, perhaps faster than anyone any of us have seen. But it would prove nothing, because he would be drawing alone. There would be no standard by which we could make our assessment."

"You have a point, counselor," Judge Huff agreed.

"Your Honor, we have considered that very thing," John said. "In fact, that is the point I tried to make when I suggested that Mrs. Scanlon could not judge the relative speed of the two men, based upon watching them perform individually. But, I believe we have crafted a demonstration that would accommodate that concern."

"What sort of demonstration would that be?" Huff asked.

"It is a demonstration suggested by my client," John replied. He walked back over to the table and picked up a pie pan and a silver dollar. He put the pie pan, upside down, on the floor. The gallery buzzed in curiosity.

"What's the pan for?" someone asked.

"What's he aimin' to do?" another questioned.

"This is how the demonstration will work," John explained. He stuck his hand out in front of him. "My client will hold his hand straight out in front of him, like so, palm down." With his other hand, John held up the silver dollar. "This coin will rest on the back of his hand, like this." John put the coin on the back of his hand so that he was now holding it out in front of him. "When he turns his hand to start for his gun, the silver dollar will fall toward the pie plate. Mr. Crockett will then draw his pistol and shoot two times, hitting his target both times before the silver coin strikes the pie plate."

John turned his hand. Then, even though he wasn't wearing a gun and holster, he acted as if he were drawing and shooting a pistol. Pointedly, the coin clanked against the pan before John could even raise his hand back up from the imaginary holster. The gallery laughed at his failure.

"Why, that's impossible," Huff said. "You couldn't even do it without a gun...let alone actually draw and shoot."

"That is true, Your Honor I couldn't, and I daresay there are few who could. Therefore, such an exhibition, if successfully performed, would clearly demonstrate my client's speed and skill with a pistol, would it not?" John asked.

"Mr. Crockett," Huff asked, leaning over his desk and looking over toward the defense table. "Can you actually do such a thing?"

"I think I can," Will replied.

"You think you can?" Huff repeated.

"I'm pretty sure I can."

"I think I'd like to see that."

"Your Honor, I strenuously object!" Haydon said. "I could see allowing him to make a demonstration with an empty pistol. But what you propose now, is giving him a loaded gun. Do you understand the gravity of this? You are actually going to let him have bullets in that gun!"

"Mr. Haydon, you are the one who said that a demonstration with an unloaded pistol would be a waste of time," Huff reminded him.

"Yes, but...to give an accused murderer a loaded gun?"

"The court will take every precaution," Judge Huff promised. "Deputy Lewis."

"Yes, Your Honor?"

While the demonstration is in progress, you will stand nearby. At all times, your pistol will be drawn, and aimed at Mr. Crockett. If he deviates one iota from the script as outlined by Mr. Woodward, you will shoot him."

Lewis smiled, broadly. "Yes sir, Your Honor, it will be my pleasure," he said.

"This court will take a five-minute recess," Huff said. "At the conclusion of that five minutes, we will reconvene out on the street in front. At that time, and in that place, Mr. Crockett will demonstrate his prowess as a marksman."

Huff rapped on the table, then got up and retired

quickly. When he was gone, the rest of the court stood, then started toward the back door, buzzing in excitement over the unexpected entertainment.

Outside of the courthouse the finishing touches were being put on the gallows. The judge had already made it clear that not only did he intend to find Will guilty today, he intended to hang him today as well.

"Mr. Crockett, I have to tell you that I am worried about this," Nora said as she, Will, and her father walked out under the watchful eye of Deputy Lewis.

"What is there to worry about?" Will asked.

"If you stop and think about it, this is a loaded situation. Even if you can do what you say, we will still have to make a case for self-defense. But if you can't do it, the prosecution will be able to claim that their case is already made."

"I'm afraid my daughter might be right," John said. "I'm now beginning to wish that I had not listened to you when you came up with this idea."

"The problem is the bell has been rung, and we can't un-ring it," Nora said. "If you back out now, it's the same as admitting defeat."

"Then, I'll just have to do it, won't I?" Will said.

By now, the entire court had reassembled in the street in front of the courthouse, to include the judge, clerk, and jury. A paper target was put on a wagon, and the wagon was pulled away, approximately fifty feet.

"Your Honor, I object," John said, when he saw the position of the wagon. "At the time of the actual shooting, the two belligerents were no more than ten feet apart. You've put this target much too far away."

"I've put it there for the safety of the observers," Huff said. "I can't see that its location should make that much difference."

"Hell, it would for me," someone in the crowd said. "I doubt if I could even hit the wagon from here, let alone that little target."

The others laughed, but Judge Huff's fixed glare forestalled any additional comments.

"Turner?" the judge said to one of the men in the crowd.

"Yes, sir?" Turner replied.

"Take all the bullets but two from your gun, then hand your pistol and belt over to the defendant."

"Your Honor, I ask that the defendant be allowed to use his own gun and holster," John said. "After all, this is no small feat we are asking of him."

"Where is his gun and holster?" Huff asked. "I will not hold the proceedings up any longer while you send someone for it."

"I have it with me, Your Honor," Nora said. Reaching into her oversized reticule, she pulled out Will's holster and pistol, tied up with its own belt.

ROBERT VAUGHAN

"Bring it to me," Huff instructed.

Nora handed it to him. The judge checked the cylinders and, satisfied that only two chambers were charged, handed it back to Nora. "Deputy Lewis," Huff said. "Draw your pistol and point it at the defendant."

Lewis drew his gun and pointed it at Will.

"Now, Miss Woodward, you may give Mr. Crockett his pistol."

Nora handed the gun and holster to Will. Will smiled at her, then strapped the rig on. He loosened the gun in his holster, a couple of times, then nodded at John. John put the pie pan on the ground in front of him, then handed Will the silver dollar. Will stretched out his hand and put the coin on the back of his hand.

"Are you ready, Mr. Crockett?" Judge Huff said.

"Wait, I can't do it like this," Will said.

The crowd buzzed at Will's answer.

"I knew he couldn't do it," someone said.

"Hell, no man could," another added.

"Then, I take it you are ready to admit defeat?" Huff asked.

"No, that's not what I meant," Will answered. He was still holding his hand out in front of him. "I meant that in order to do this I need an element of danger. Nothing makes a gunman faster than the thought that if he doesn't succeed, he'll be killed."

"Do you have a proposal as to how we may add that element of danger?" Huff asked.

"I do," Will answered with a smile. He looked over at the deputy, who was still pointing his pistol at Will. "Lewis, if I don't pull my gun and shoot the target before you hear the coin hit the pie pan, I want you to shoot me."

"What?" Nora asked. Her incredulous response was met with a buzz of excitement and disbelief from those in the crowd.

"Mister, you gone plumb loco? Lewis would like nothing more than to shoot you," someone said.

"Yeah, and how do you know he won't start shooting even before he hears the coin clank?" another asked.

"What'll I do, Judge?" Lewis asked, unsure of himself.

"You heard the man, Deputy," Huff replied. "If he doesn't get his two shots off before the coin hits the pie pan, shoot him."

Lewis smiled broadly. "Yes, sir, Your Honor. I'll do that gladly!"

"Will! Have you gone crazy?" Nora asked in alarm.

Will looked over at her and winked.

"Alright, ever'one back out of the way," Huff said. "Mr. Crockett, anytime you're ready."

At the time everyone started filing out of the courtroom, the carpenters were still working on the gallows. But word spread quickly as to what was about to happen, so the carpenters abandoned their saws and hammers and came down to watch. At the same time, drinkers left the saloon, clerks and customers quit the stores, men came from the livery and the freight company, housewives abandoned their washing, and children ran from the school to see the show. Like ants swarming to a sugar cube, the crowd in front of the courthouse swelled to well over two hundred people. In fact, the only citizens of the town who weren't present, were those few who were too sick, too old, or too young. And now, as they waited for the demonstration, the whispered buzz of excitement stilled, and the crowd became absolutely silent.

A sign squeaked in the wind.

Time itself waited.

Then, suddenly, Will turned his hand, and the crowd drew a collective breath as the coin started falling toward the pie pan. In the blink of an eye, the gun was in Will's hand. It cracked once...twice...then the coin hit the pan. It was all over before the crowd realized that Will's first shot had not been at the target, but at the gun in Lewis's hand. It was not until Lewis shouted out in pain and anger that everyone realized what happened.

"You...you son of a bitch, you shot me!" Lewis shouted, holding his hand. A trickle of blood was running down from his middle finger. It had been creased just enough to make him drop the gun, though the finger had not been crushed by the impact of the bullet.

"He hit the target dead center," someone called from down by the wagon. That had been Will's second shot.

There was a spontaneous burst of applause, silenced only when Judge Huff was able to regain control.

"Deputy, retrieve your pistol," Huff said.

Grumbling, Lewis did as the judge asked.

"Now, if you would, please escort the prisoner back into the court."

Chapter Seventeen

As the court members and gallery filed back into the community building, they were still expressing awe and disbelief over what they had just witnessed.

"In all my borned days, I ain't never seen nothin' like that."

"I didn't think it was humanly possible for anyone to be that fast."

"Sheriff Townsend was fast, but he wasn't nowhere near to being that fast."

Even the members of the jury, men who were supposed to be impartial witnesses, expressed their amazement over what they had just seen.

Judge Huff called the court back to order, then directed that the trial continue. John Woodward was invited to give his summation.

"Gentlemen of the jury, the law is very clear," John

began. "In order to bring a verdict of guilty, you must establish a trinity of events. You must establish that Crockett had the opportunity to kill Townsend...that he had the means to kill Townsend...and finally, the motive to kill Townsend.

"You heard Mrs. Scanlon testify that Crockett and Townsend stood face to face on the front porch of The Whistle Stop Saloon. Defense will stipulate, therefore, that this did present Crockett with the opportunity to kill Townsend. But I ask you to remember this, Crockett's horse was killed out in the middle of the desert, and he was forced to walk nearly twenty miles in blistering heat... without water...to get here. I submit to you therefore, that this was an opportunity born of fate, not of aforethought. You are trying a case of first degree murder. And, without malice and aforethought, there...can...be...no...conviction.

"Secondly, we must consider if he had the means to kill Sheriff Townsend. Defense will also stipulate that yes; Mr. Crockett did have the means. In fact, we just witnessed a remarkable demonstration in which Mr. Crockett proved to us that he had the means to best Townsend in a gunfight, even if Townsend drew first. If Townsend drew first, there...can...be...no...conviction.

"It is Mr. Crockett's contention that Townsend did draw first, and we have no direct eyewitnesses who can testify to the contrary."

Here, John paused and stared hard at each member of the jury, all of whom were sitting spell bound by his oratory. "If there is the slightest chance that Crockett might be telling the truth...then that alone is sufficient to cast a shadow of doubt over his guilt. Remember that, because if there is the slightest doubt, there...can...be... no...conviction.

"And now, to the third branch of our trinity. We have discussed opportunity and means. Let us now discuss motive. All three elements must be considered in bringing about a guilty verdict. And, while we will stipulate as to opportunity and means, the lack of motive is glaring. What was Will Crockett's motive? Why would he have walked twenty miles across a barren desert just to kill Sheriff Townsend?

"The answer is, he wouldn't have. The only reason he killed Sheriff Townsend was because Sheriff Townsend was trying to kill him. And that isn't motive, that is self-defense. And if Crockett acted in self-defense, there... can...be...no... conviction."

As in each of the previous times, John set the words of his mantra apart, allowing them to sink in. After an extended silence, he resumed his summation.

"And finally, before you render your verdict, I ask each and every one of you to look deep into your inner souls. Consider all that I have told you. The burden of proof is upon the prosecution. If there is the slightest chance that you believe Mr. Crockett's story...that you believe he was braced on the front porch of The Whistle Stop Saloon...and that he did not draw his gun until he perceived his life to be in mortal danger, then there... can...be...no...conviction.

"Thank you."

Nora was smiling proudly at her father as he returned to his chair behind the table for the defense. Will leaned over to him.

"You've done a good job for me, Mr. Woodward," he said. "Regardless of how this comes out, I couldn't have asked for a better lawyer."

"Thank you, my boy," John said. His eyes were misted over with tears. "Odd, how things work out, isn't it? I am trying hard to save your life, and in so doing, I may have just saved my own."

"Prosecution, your closing remarks?" Judge Huff invited.

Standing, Oscar Haydon looked over toward the defense table. "Before I address this court, Your Honor, let me first congratulate Mr. Woodward on the fine and spirited defense he has put up for Will Crockett. To those of us who have grown accustomed to seeing him drunk, it is heartening to see him sober."

"That was a backhanded compliment if I have ever

heard one," Nora said under her breath.

"I don't think it was a compliment, dear," John replied. "Wait for the other shoe to drop. Mr. Haydon is far too calculating for empty compliments."

Haydon approached the jury.

"Some of you may have wondered how a man of John Woodward's obvious intelligence and talent could have fallen so far.

"To answer that question, we must go back to a trial that took place in this very building, two years ago. At that trial our positions were reversed. Woodward, until then, a fine, upstanding lawyer and leading citizen of Watson, was prosecuting. I, the younger and more inexperienced lawyer, was defending.

"The defendants were Sheriff Townsend, and Rhiny Brown. You see, gentlemen of the jury, Nora Woodward thought Ernest Townsend would make a fine husband, so, she threw herself at him, only to have him reject her. And, as the saying goes, hell hath no fury like a woman scorned.

"Nora Woodward then took revenge upon the sheriff by accusing him of raping her. But, her fury was so great that she didn't stop with Townsend. Her accusation took in Mr. Rhiny Brown as well. Now, rape is a foul crime, and society is justifiably harsh with the perpetrators of such an act. But, because of that very harshness, we must also be certain that the accusation is true. Alas, the charges brought against Sheriff Townsend and Mr. Brown by Nora Woodward were proven, in this very court, and with this very judge," Haydon pointed to Huff, "to be false. Ernest Townsend and Rhiny Brown were exonerated.

"John Woodward had fought hard to uphold the honor of his daughter, but he was fighting an uphill battle, because truth has a way of winning out over even the cleverest and most skilled lawyer. Unable to face the humiliation his daughter had brought down upon them, John Woodward took to drink. The result of his failing battle with demon rum is the poor wretch we all know today.

"You may be wondering, gentlemen of the jury, why I told you this story. I told it, not to further embarrass Mr. Woodward, but to supply you with that missing element in the trinity that the defense counsel so clearly laid out for us. If you will recall, Mr. Woodward stipulated as to means and opportunity. But where, he asked, was the motive?

"The motive, gentlemen, is right here."

Dramatically, Haydon pointed to Nora Woodward.

"Will Crockett killed Sheriff Townsend to avenge this vindictive woman."

"What?" Nora shouted out loud.

"Objection!" John yelled.

Huff banged his gavel.

"Mr. Woodward, Miss Woodward, silence during summation."

"Your Honor, this isn't summation, this is a new charge. None of the information the prosecutor spoke of was introduced during the trial." John looked at Haydon. "Are you accusing my daughter of hiring this man to kill Sheriff Townsend?"

"No, not at all," Haydon said quickly. "Indeed, I am positive she is innocent of it. I contend that Crockett did it on his own, without the prior consent of Nora Woodward, perhaps in hopes of winning her favor. She is after all, a very beautiful young woman."

"Your Honor, this is preposterous!" John said. "Neither my daughter nor I had ever met, nor even heard of Mr. Crockett before this trial began."

Haydon looked at the men in the jury. "Is it preposterous, gentlemen? Suppose I told you that on the very next day after Sheriff Townsend was killed...Nora Woodward was seen kissing Will Crockett through the bars of his jail cell by none other than Judge Huff himself?"

"That's true," Huff said. "I did see them kissing."

After the reaction from the gallery, Haydon continued his summation. "Despite Miss Woodward's questionable background, I don't think anyone is ready to believe that she is a woman of such loose morals that she would kiss a man whom she met for the first time."

"My daughter is not a woman of loose morals, and you know that!" John shouted in anger.

"Indeed, I do know that, sir," Haydon replied, almost patronizingly. "That is why I submit that there had to be some earlier collusion...either inferred by your daughter... or imagined by Will Crockett. I am willing to believe that it was imagined by Will Crockett. But in any case, it does provide the motive you so ardently suggested was missing. And in so doing, satisfies the requirements for the jury to find a verdict of guilty of first degree murder." Haydon turned back toward the jury. "And with that, gentlemen of the jury, I rest my case."

Oscar Haydon's fiery and scathing accusation, stunned the gallery, and they sat in absolute silence as Haydon returned to his seat.

Judge Huff began his instructions.

"You have heard the case as presented by both defense and prosecution. It is not necessary for you to consider who killed Sheriff Townsend, for that issue is not in contention. Clearly, Sheriff Townsend was killed by Will Crockett. The only thing you must decide is whether this killing was murder or self-defense.

"If, somehow, you can overcome the clear evidence that Sheriff Townsend's gun was still in his holster when he died, and actually believe he drew first, then it is self-defense, and you must acquit.

"On the other hand, if you think that the fact that Sheriff Townsend's gun was still in its holster is compelling physical evidence that he couldn't have started his draw, it is murder, and you must convict.

"The first consideration, it seems to me, requires a suspension of belief. The second consideration requires merely the acceptance of the preponderance of evidence.

"You may now retire to consider the verdict."

"My God!" John said under his breath. "Huff has just all but ordered the jury to return a verdict of guilty."

The jury met in the farthest corner of the room to deliberate. Deputy Lewis stood guard to keep away the many people who wanted to offer their own suggestions. In the meantime, Will, John, and Nora, waited at the defense table.

"I want to apologize to you, Mr. Crockett, for having your name dragged through my own personal slime and mud," John said.

"I don't think anyone will actually believe Haydon's claim that there is a connection," Will said.

"On the contrary," John said. "There is an element of truth in what he said. When Townsend and Brown...," he looked at Nora, then paused. Nora reached across the table to put her hand on his.

"You can say it, Pa," she said. "When they raped me."

John nodded. "When those two monsters raped my daughter, they thought they could get away with it because they were representatives of the law. I, on the other hand, was a pompous, arrogant fool. I was absolutely positive that the law they proposed to uphold, the very law that I revered, would turn upon those despoilers of the sacred trust and take care of them."

"That's the trial Haydon was talking about?" Will asked.

"Yes," John said. "I lost the case, and Townsend and Brown went free. I failed my own daughter when she needed me most." John hung his head in shame, and a tear began to slide down his cheek.

"You didn't fail me, Pa. The jury was frightened of them," Nora said. "We never had a chance with the jury."

"I'm talking about after the trial," John said, and he put his other hand on top of Nora's to squeeze it. "I failed you when I started drinking. I've no excuse for the way I have behaved these past two years. When you needed me most, is when I was at my worst. I can only beg you to forgive me...and promise you that, beginning now, I am going to make every effort to regain my life...and my dignity."

Father and daughter were in the midst of an embrace when someone called out.

"The jury is coming back!"

Will looked toward the corner of the room where

the jury had been meeting, and saw that the twelve men were returning to the area that had been set aside as the jury box.

"Order in the court!" the clerk shouted, and the milling, buzzing throng of people quickly took their seats to see what verdict the jury would deliver.

"Defendant will rise," Huff said.

Will stood.

"Face the jury."

Will turned toward the jury.

"Gentlemen of the jury, have you reached a verdict?" Huff asked.

"Yeah, we have."

Huff glared at the foreman of the jury.

"You will address this court with respect," Huff demanded.

"Oh, uh, yeah, I mean, yes sir...uh...yes Your Honor."

"Publish the verdict, please."

"What?" the foreman asked, confused by the term.

"Please tell the court your verdict."

"Well, by a vote of nine to three, we find the defendant not guilty."

The gallery reaction was immediate as dozens of voices sounded.

"Damn, John, you done it!" someone from the gallery shouted.

"No," John said, speaking under his breath. He was shaking his head. "This isn't right. There's something wrong, here."

The loudest voice of all was coming from Haydon. He continued to shout until Will was able to hear what he was saying.

"Objection, Your Honor, objection! The verdict must be unanimous!"

"Is that right?" Will asked. "Does it have to be unanimous?"

"I'm afraid so."

"Your Honor, I call for a mistrial!" Haydon shouted.

"What does that mean? A mistrial?" Will asked.

"It means we have to do this all over."

Huff began banging his gavel, and he continued to bang it until the courtroom was absolutely quiet. When you could hear a pin drop, he looked over toward the jury.

"Is there any chance of the twelve of you coming up with a unanimous verdict?"

The foreman shook his head. "There ain't a chance in hell, Judge. They's nine of 'em says he ain't guilty, and they ain't goin' to change their minds, no matter what we say to 'em." The foreman then looked over at Will. "But then, they's three of us says Crockett is guilty as hell, and we want to see the son of a bitch hung."

"Very well, this jury is dismissed," Judge Huff said.

"Your Honor, you are declaring a mistrial?" John asked.

Huff looked first at Woodward, then at Haydon. "Declaring a mistrial would mean empaneling a new jury. And, like as not, we'd have the same problem with them as we had with this jury. No mistrial."

"No mistrial? Your Honor, you mean you are going to let the verdict, as brought by the jury, stand?" Haydon asked.

Nora smiled broadly, and spontaneously hugged Will. "We won!" she said.

"No, I don't think so," John said in a quiet voice. He held his hand out. "Wait."

"I have decided to dismiss the jury and render a summary judgment," Huff said. "My summary judgment is, guilty."

"What? Your Honor, you can't do that!" John shouted. "I'm going to appeal!"

"You can appeal all you want, Mr. Woodward, but it will be too late to do your client any good. Mr. Crockett, I find you guilty, and I sentence you to hang by the neck until dead. That sentence to be carried out at four o'clock this afternoon. That is...," Huff looked up at the wall clock. "Two and one half-hours from now. May God have mercy on your soul."

Chapter Eighteen

"Stop that!" the little girl in pigtails cried.

The young boy who had tied the girl's pigtails together, ran away, giggling in delight.

"Mama, look what Cody did," the little girl tattled.

"Cody, if you don't behave yourself, I'm going to make you go home, and you won't get to see the hanging," Cody's mother scolded.

"No, mama, don't make me go home. I want to stay and watch," Cody protested.

"Then stop pestering your little sister," the woman ordered.

"All right, I'll leave the little baby alone," Cody said sarcastically, sticking his tongue out at his little sister, who stuck her tongue back at him. Leaving her and his mother, Cody hurried over to join another group of young boys, all of whom were occupying a position in the very front of the crowd.

"You think he'll make a noise when he gets hung?" one of the boys asked.

"Nah, he can't make no noise," one of the others answered. "The rope'll be chokin' 'im, so he can't say a word."

"How much longer?"

"Don't know. Not much."

The gallows the boys were standing by was an unpainted, fresh-smelling structure built of new wood. A stairway of thirteen steps led to the gallows floor. It stood high and occupied a prominent position in the middle of the street, right in front of the community center where, earlier, Will Crockett had been tried, convicted, and sentenced to hang.

It was not quite three-thirty, but already the crowd was thick and jostling for position. There were men in suits, shirtsleeves, and overalls, women in long dresses and bonnets, and children, not only Cody, his sister, and the group of fascinated boys, but other, younger children who threaded in and out of the crowd as they chased one another around the gallows. A few enterprising vendors were selling lemonade, beer, pretzels, popcorn, and sweet rolls.

Half a block away from the gallows, in the Watson jail, Lewis, who by now had been given the position of sheriff, was standing at the front window looking out onto the street. Behind him, on the bunk in his cell, Will sat, calmly paring an apple. One long, connected peel hung down from the apple.

"Hey, look at this," he said enthusiastically. This may be the longest single peel I've ever done."

"What? Why are you doing that?" Nora asked in an exasperated voice. "I can't believe this. They are about to hang you and you...you are talking about a long apple peel."

Both Nora and John were in the cell with Will, allowed this privilege by Judge Huff because they were his lawyers. Nora was standing by the window that looked out over the alley behind the jail. John was sitting on an overturned water bucket.

"Well, long apple peels can sometimes pay off," Will said easily. "I won a dollar once for having the longest peel. I beat Frank James by almost a full inch."

"Stop it!" Nora said, turning toward him. "Don't you understand what is about to happen to you?"

Will finished the peel, then lay it on the bunk beside him. He looked up at Nora.

"Of course I know what is about to happen to me, Nora," he said. "I'm about to be hanged."

"And you aren't concerned?"

"Not particularly."

"I don't understand that. You must be insane." Practically wringing her hands, Nora turned to her father. "Pa, we used the wrong tactic. We should have pled him not guilty by reason of insanity."

"I'm not insane, Nora," Will said, his voice still calm. "But you have to realize that I have faced the prospect of instant death for nearly all of my adult life. First in the war, and then in the life I have lived since the war. You can't be worrying about it all the time. So, I have made a conscious decision to treat death for what it is, a fact of life that is always there, waiting for all of us."

"That's an abstract concept," Nora said. "What I am talking about is real. It is right here, right now."

Will looked over at the clock on the wall of the sheriff's office. "No," he said, shaking his head. "It isn't here yet. I've got nearly half-an-hour remaining."

"Half an hour? Half an hour? Half an hour is nothing!"

"That's where you are wrong. The next half an hour is the rest of my life."

"No, I just can't accept that!" Nora wailed.

"Let's not give up hope yet, honey," John said, speaking for the first time. "I've sent a telegram to Governor Blalock. In it, I made it clear, in no uncertain terms, that this trial was a total miscarriage of justice. And, you might be interested to know that Oscar Haydon joined in the appeal."

174

"Haydon did?" Will asked.

John shook his head. "Haydon is a good man. He prosecuted as vigorously as he could, because that was his job. But in the final analysis, he is a man of principle and ethical courage. He, too, believes the case should have been declared a mistrial."

"Why haven't we heard from the governor?" Nora asked. "We should have heard from him by now. Are you sure he hasn't answered?"

"Honey, as soon as he answers, we will know. Lenny, down at Western Union, will run it down here immediately."

"Suppose Governor Blalock does grant us a stay, can we count on Judge Huff to abide by it?" Nora asked.

"He'll have to. If the governor orders a stay, Huff will have no choice but to comply," John said. "Especially as Oscar Haydon backs me on this."

The front door opened then and the hangman came in. He was smiling broadly.

"I'll bet there are three hundred people out there, waiting for the show," Lighthouse said to Lewis and the others as he walked over to the coffeepot to pour himself a cup of coffee.

"That's what you call it? A show?" Nora asked.

"I call it a show, because that's what it is," Lighthouse said, coming over to stand just outside the cell. "Whenever somebody sees a hangin', why, that's somethin' that will stay with them for the rest of their lives. It's entertaining and educational. And it stars just two people. The hangman," he made a slight bow, "that's me. And the person gettin' hung." He swept one arm toward Will. "That's him."

"You actually enjoy this, don't you?" Nora asked incredulously.

"Oh, indeed I do, madam, indeed I do," Lighthouse said. "There's no greater satisfaction in life than for someone to take pleasure in the work they do. I take pleasure in my work, and I'm very good at it."

"What's good about it?" John asked.

"The dignity of the moment," Lighthouse said. He looked again at Will, who, as yet, had not joined the conversation. "When I send you off to see your maker, Mr. Crockett, you can be sure that I'll do it in a dignified manner."

"Yeah, thanks," Will answered. "I'd been worried about that," he added, sarcastically.

"Hey, Lighthouse," Lewis called back from the front of the jail. "Here comes Judge Huff."

"Wonder what he wants?" Lighthouse asked.

"Pa! Maybe the stay has come through from the governor," Nora suggested excitedly.

"I don't know. It could be possible," John said, showing some hope.

Will, who had now cut his apple into sections, began to eat it. He made no comment as to the possibility that the governor may have responded to John's telegram, nor did he show any reaction.

When Huff came in, he walked straight over to the jail cell where he stood, alongside Lighthouse, just outside the cell. "Woodward, did you and Haydon wire the governor behind my back?" he asked.

"Yes, we did," John said. "Has there been an answer?"

Huff chuckled. "Oh yes, there's been an answer. It seems that the governor is an overnight guest for dinner at a nearby ranch, and they won't be able to deliver the message to him until he returns tomorrow. Looks like it's going to reach him too late to make any difference."

"Too late? What do you mean, too late?"

"Crockett's going to hang today," Huff said.

"Judge, surely you aren't going to go through with it now? You have the authority to delay this until tomorrow," John said. "I beg of you to do so. Give us a chance to hear from the governor."

"I have no intention of changing my ruling. The execution takes place at four o'clock, as planned," Judge Huff said. He pulled a watch from his pocket and examined it. "That's less than fifteen minutes now. Sheriff Lewis?"

"Yes, sir?"

"I suggest you get this prisoner down to the gallows. Mr. Lighthouse, it is time for you to go to work."

"It will be my honor," Lighthouse said.

Chapter Nineteen

"You would be Mr. Edwards?" Gid said as he dismounted at the livery.

"Yes," Edwards replied. "Come to see the hanging, did you?"

Gid noticed with some satisfaction that the tone and expression in Carl Edwards' voice denoted his disapproval of the event.

"No, I came to stop it," Gid said.

Edwards looked at Gid with a questioning expression. "You're going to stop it? Now, Mister, with the law and the entire town standing out there waiting for their show, just how the hell do you plan on stopping it all by yourself?"

"I won't be by myself."

"Oh? And just who is going to help you?"

"Suzy Jenkins told me that you would help me."

"Who are you?" Edwards asked.

"I'm Gideon Crockett."

"You're Will Crockett's brother."

"Yes. Was Suzy telling the truth, Mr. Edwards? Will you help me?"

"It depends on what you want me to do," Edwards said. "If you plan to charge into that crowd, blazing away, you're going to have to get yourself another man. But if you've got some more practical way of my helping you, yeah, you can count on me."

Gid smiled at Edwards. "Good," he said. "We can start by you selling me a horse and saddle."

Edwards nodded. "That seems easy enough for me to do."

"There's more," Gid said. "You don't have to participate with me if you don't want to, but I do want you to help me gather what we will need."

As Gid explained his plan, a big smile spread across Edwards' face.

"Yeah," Edwards said enthusiastically. "Yeah, you can count me in for that."

Back in the jail at that moment, Lewis walked over to the cell and opened the door.

"All right, John, Miss Woodward, you folks, come on out of there now," he said. "Your visitin' time is over."

With a dolorous expression on his face, John looked

at Will. Hesitantly, he stuck out his hand. "Good bye, Mr. Crockett. I'm sorry I couldn't have done more for you."

Will shook it. "You've done all you could, and I've been grateful," he said.

Nora approached Will, started to hug him, then, unable to face him, turned away with a little sob. John was providing what comfort he could for his daughter as they left the jail.

"Turn around," Lewis ordered, and as Will did so, Lewis tied his hands behind his back. "All right," he said. "Let's go."

With a shotgun poking into his back, Will walked the half-block that separated the jail from the gallows. As he passed through the crowd of onlookers, he studied their faces. He saw pity in some, and horror in others, but morbid fascination in most. He smiled at a little girl with pigtails. Frightened, the little girl turned her face into her mother's skirt.

"Get up there," Lewis growled, prodding him with sharp pokes in the back from the shotgun.

"Do you want a hood?" Lighthouse asked, holding up a piece of black cloth.

"No," Will replied. "When I get to hell, I want to look the devil right square in the face."

"Oohh," a woman in the front gasped at hearing such blasphemy.

In the distance a hawk called, and Will looked toward him and saw him flying free. Then an amazing thing happened. Will felt that, somehow, he and that bird had exchanged places, so that he was the one flying around, looking down on the proceedings. He felt totally detached from what was going on.

He reconnected with himself though, when he saw Gid coming toward the gallows, riding one horse and leading another. There was someone just behind Gid and at first Will was a little concerned, then he realized that they were together.

Gid, and the man with him were both smoking cigars and holding something in their hands. Will saw the man with Gid touch the smoldering cigar to one of the objects in his hand, then throw it. That was when he realized that the man with Gid was carrying several sticks of blasting powder.

As Gid was coming up behind the crowd, no one but Will had even noticed him. Therefore, when the first stick exploded, no one was expecting it, and there were several screams of surprise and fright. Almost immediately on the heels of the first explosion, there was a second, then a third. The street began emptying of all the spectators even as Gid and the other man with him continued their methodical approach. Will didn't know who Gid's helper was, but he welcomed his participation in this surprise appearance.

Casually, and with a big grin spread across his face, Gid tossed a stick of dynamite right in front of the gallows. It's sputtering fuse cleared out what was left of the crowd. He tossed still another stick up onto the gallows floor. It rolled across the floor to Will's feet, then stopped. Will could hear the fuse sparking, and smell the burning cordite. Lewis and the hangman were both on the gallows floor with Win.

"Holy shit!" Lewis shouted, jumping off the edge of the gallows. Lighthouse, with his own cry of alarm, was right behind him.

"Get on," Gid said easily, leading the second horse right up to the gallows.

Will's hands were still tied behind him, but the height of the gallows made it easy for him to just walk over and slip down onto the saddle.

"Hurry," Will said. "The fuse is almost down."

"Don't worry," Gid replied with a chuckle. "That one isn't real." Gid rode away from the gallows then, still leading the second horse because Will, with his hands tied behind him, couldn't hold the reins.

They were no more than a few feet away when the stick of blasting powder Gid had tossed onto the gallows exploded. It went up with a roar, scattering shattered pieces of the lumber all over the center of town.

"Damn!" Will shouted, as chunks of wood, some of it rather large, rained down on them. "I thought you said that one wasn't real!"

"I must've gotten them mixed up," Gid said easily.

"That's a hell of a thing to get mixed up."

"You want to stay around here and talk about it, big brother? Or do you want to get the hell out of here?"

"Let's get the hell out of here," Will agreed, and using his legs for leverage, he held on as well as he could while Gid led them both out of town at a full gallop.

"Do you see anything from there?" Gid called. Will, who was clinging to the top of the telegraph pole looked back in the direction from which they had come.

"I'm not exactly riding the back of a hawk up here Gid. I don't have that much better of a view than you do."

"Yeah, well I don't see anything from down here," Gid said. "I figured sure they would be after us by now."

"Not if Lewis has to get the posse together," Will replied. "He couldn't pour piss out of a boot if he had the instructions written on the heel." Will leaned around the pole and, using his knife, cut the telegraph wire. It fell to the ground with a twang, then Will climbed back down.

"There," he said. "This is the third section of wire we've removed. It'll take them a day or two to repair it. By the time they can send out any telegraph messages about us, we'll be well out of here. What do you say we head west, toward Arizona?"

Gid took a drink from his canteen, then screwed the top back on and hooked it across his saddle pommel.

"All right," Gid agreed. "But not until we go through Gold Hill."

"Gold Hill? Why do you want to go there?"

"For the same reason I wanted you to meet me there, instead of me coming to Thornburg," Gid said. He opened his shirt pocket and took out the little peanut-sized nugget. "For this," he said, handing the nugget to his brother.

Will looked at it. "Damn, Gid," he said. "This is gold."

"It damn sure is," Will said as a wide grin spread across his face. "I told you I was goin' prospectin' while you were going to be gallivanting around back in Missouri. Well, I did go, and this is what I found. This...and a whole lot more like this."

"How much more?" Will asked.

"Well, if what Mr. Bell says is true, we might be talking in the neighborhood of fifty to a hundred thousand dollars or more."

"That's a pretty good neighborhood to be in," Will said.

"Yeah," Gid said. "That's what I was thinking."

"It won't do us much good, though, if we're picked up soon as we ride into Gold Hill," Will said.

"You've never been to Gold Hill, so the chances are

you won't even be recognized," Gid said. "Besides, there's no posse comin' after us, and, like you said, we've cut the wire in a couple of places. It'll be a couple of days before word can even get out, and that's all we'll need."

"Then, lead on, McDuff, lead on," Will said as he swung into his saddle.

"McDuff," Gid said. "Yeah, I remember him. He was that red headed guy from Springfield, wasn't he?"

Will laughed. "Yeah, something like that."

Chapter Twenty

The two brothers spent the night on the trail, and rode into Gold Hill early the next morning. As they passed by the cluster of small houses that sat just on the outskirts of town, a couple of women were talking back and forth as they hung out their wash. When they heard the hollow clump of hoofbeats, they halted their conversation and looked curiously over at Will and Gid. Smiling, Will touched the brim of his hat and nodded.

From those two houses, and the dozen or so others nearby, came the aroma of breakfast: bacon, coffee, eggs, and freshly baked biscuits.

Gid felt his stomach rumble with hunger.

By the time they reached the downtown area, a few of the merchants were already beginning their day's commerce. The hardware dealer raised dust with a vigorous use of his broom as he swept his front porch, while the grocer was using a chalkboard to post distress prices on the produce he had to move that day, or lose by spoilage. Both merchants nodded at the two brothers as they rode by.

A derelict, just awakening from his overnight drunk, pissed on the side of the leather goods store, totally unconcerned about his public exposure.

A dog scratched his fleas.

A prospector riding one mule and leading another plodded down the street.

"Nobody has gotten excited over seeing us yet," Will suggested as they stopped in front of the Gold Hill Corral. The liveryman, still holding a cup of coffee came out to greet them. Wearing bib overalls and no shirt, he reeked, not only with body odor, but a few other, unidentifiable foul smells.

"How long?" he asked, as he took the reins.

"We'll do it a day at a time until we know," Gid replied. He paid the fifty cents it required to board and feed both horses for one day and night.

"Rub them down," Will said.

"Always do," the stableman said. "It's part of the job."

When they stepped back outside, Gid pointed to a building just up the street. "That's Little Man Keller's Café," he said. "Why don't we have breakfast? If anybody is going to know anything about us, that's where we're going to find out."

Will chuckled. "Gid, if I didn't know you better, I'd say that was a good idea. But I know damn well that all you're thinking about right now is your stomach."

"Well, I am hungry," Gid agreed. "And you are, too, if you'd just admit it. Wait until you eat here. Little Man puts out the best breakfast I ever tasted."

"Every breakfast is the best breakfast you ever tasted," Will teased. As they approached the café, the aromas awakened Will's appetite as well, but he wasn't about to let Gid know that.

When Little Man saw Gid come into his café, he smiled broadly and hurried over to meet him.

"Hello, my friend!" Little Man said, shaking Gid's hand. "It's good to see you again."

"Hello, Little Man," Gid said. "I was telling my...uh, friend...here, what a good breakfast you put out." Gid introduced Will as his friend, rather than brother, just in case word was out to look for two brothers.

"Coming from one with your appetite, I appreciate the compliment," Little Man said. "But if your friend eats like you do, I'm afraid I'll have to put on an extra shift in the kitchen."

Some of the nearby diners, particularly those who had been present the last time Gid had breakfast here, and who remembered Gid's prodigious appetite, laughed and told the others what Little Man was talking about.

"You don't have to explain it to me, I've seen him eat before," Will said. "And believe me, I don't eat like he does. In fact, I'm not sure anyone eats like he does."

"Have a seat, gentlemen," Little Man said. "I'll bring you some coffee, then get the cook started on your breakfast. In fact, I'll probably have to help him."

Will and Gid took a table in the back of the room sitting with their backs to the wall, and in such a way as to afford them a view of the entire café and all its entrances.

"All right, Little Brother, this is your deal. So, what's your plan?" Will asked quietly as they took their seat.

"I thought we would go down to the assayer's office as soon as it opens," Gid replied. "By now he'll have the final report on what I brought in, and we'll be able to convert what I left with him to cash, over at the bank. That's one thousand dollars, less the hundred I got from Bell. Then, we'll go up to my claim and see what's there."

Will chuckled. "I've done a lot of things in my life, but I never thought I would be digging around like a miner."

"Miner?" Gid shook his head. "No, Will, that's the beauty of it. I didn't have to dig this stuff out. It was lying around loose, scattered in the dry chute of a creek bed. I just picked it up."

Little Man came over to their table then, carrying two cups and a coffeepot.

"Little Man, what time does the assayer's office open this morning?" Gid asked.

Little Man looked up at Gid with an expression of surprise on his face.

"The assayer's office?"

"Yes, Mr. Bell. What time does he open?"

"Oh, my friend, you mean you haven't heard?"

"Heard? Heard what?"

"It's a terrible thing. Milton Bell was killed a couple of days ago."

"How?"

"He was murdered," Little Man said.

"Any idea who did it? Or why he was murdered?" Gid asked.

Little Man shook his head. "Nobody knows who it was, but ever'one thinks it was robbery. They say he had nearly a thousand dollars' worth of gold in his office."

"Now, how would anyone know that?" Gid asked.

Little Man shrugged. "I don't know. I just know what ever'one is sayin'."

"What about his records?" Gid asked. "I filed on a claim a few days ago."

"Oh, you won't have any problem with that," Little Man said. "All of his records have been transferred to the land office. All you have to do is go down there with your claim number."

190

"That's good to know," Gid said.

"Have you got your claim number?" Will asked after Little Man left the table.

"Yep. I've got it right here," Gid said, patting the same shirt pocket where he was keeping his gold nugget. "We'll go down there after breakfast."

A moment later, Little Man began bringing out the first round of the boys' breakfast. Gid didn't disappoint Little Man, nor any of Little Man's patrons. His breakfast was of legendary proportions and, as he was putting it away, Will overheard someone at one of the other tables.

"I told you so. Now pay up."

"I would never have believed you, if I hadn't seen it with my own eyes," an awed voice responded as he pulled out a silver dollar to pay off his wager.

After breakfast, Will and Gid started toward the land office to check on Gid's claim. They just stepped out of the café when they heard an excited shout.

"Coach is comin' in! Coach is comin' in!" a male voice called.

At the far end of the street, a coach, pulled by a team of six horses, came sliding around the corner then up the street. There was no real need to hold the team at a gallop, and indeed, when the coach was out on the road, the horses maintained a comfortable trot. But as the coming and going of the stage coach was generally an event of some interest to small, isolated towns such as Gold Hill, the drivers invariably arrived and departed at a gallop.

Followed by half-a-dozen running kids, the horses pulled the coach at a very rapid clip up the street, hooves pounding and wheels whirling, and throwing back a rooster tail from the hard-packed dirt of Gold Hill's Main Street.

"Whoa! Whoa!" the driver called to his team as the coach approached the coach depot, which was just next door to Little Man's. The driver hauled back on the reins and pushed the brake lever forward with his right foot. The wheels began to skid, and the horses came to a shuddering stop, then stood there, blowing hard, shaking their manes and stomping their feet, trying to bleed off the energy that had sustained them for the last several miles.

"Gold Hill, folks!" the driver called. He tied off his reins, then climbed down. "This here is Gold Hill!"

The driver opened the coach door and four passengers stepped out of the stage. None of the passengers meant anything to Gid, but when Will saw them, he drew a gasp of surprise.

"I'll be damned," he said.

"What is it?"

Will pointed to two of the passengers. "That's John and Nora Woodward," he said.

Neither John nor Nora had eaten their breakfast, so, after introductions, the four of them returned to Little Man's. Gid ordered a stack of pancakes for himself.

"Gid, don't tell me you're still hungry," Will said.

"Well, I'm not, really. But I don't like to see anyone have to eat alone. Are you going to eat that bacon?" he asked, when he saw Nora push it aside.

"No," Nora answered. "Do you want it?"

"Not really, but I reckon it would be a shame for it to go to waste," Gid said, reaching for it. He ate it in three bites.

"I'm really surprised to see you here. Pleased, but surprised," Will said. "How did you know where to find me?"

"The first day we met you said you were on your way to Gold Hill to meet your brother when someone shot your horse," John said.

"That's right, I was. Yeah, I guess I do remember telling you that," Will said. He took a swallow of his coffee and studied John over the rim of his coffee. "I guess I just didn't think you would remember it."

"It's easy to see why you would think that I wouldn't remember," John said. "As I recall, I was pretty hungover that day. But then, I've been hungover every day now for nearly two years. Except for today."

"So, you knew where to look for me. The next question is, why have you come after me? I hope you don't have some notion of trying to talk me into going back."

ROBERT VAUGHAN

Nora laughed, and John shook his head. "Heavens no," he said. "I'd never do that to you. Especially since I have this," John said, taking a paper from his jacket pocket.

"What is that?" Will asked.

"It's a telegram from Governor Blaylock, granting you a stay of execution, pending a new trial.

Will laughed. "That's nice, but if Gid hadn't taken a hand, the governor's stay would have arrived too late. I am curious, though. How did you get the message? We cut the wires as we left Watson."

John chuckled. "Believe me, I know...I tried to send a telegram ahead to Gold Hill to tell you about the stay. The truth is, Will, this wire arrived before you left. Judge Huff knew about it all along, but he decided to ignore it. Instead, he came up with that cock and bull story about the governor being out of reach."

"Why would he do that?" Will asked.

John shook his head. "He obviously wanted you dead. Have you ever crossed paths with Judge Huff?"

"Not that I know of."

"Well, for some reason, he seems to have it in for you."

"I don't know what you did when you got back from Missouri, Big Brother, but you sure got a heap of folks mad at both of us. First, those fellas back in Thornburg tried to kill you, then they came after me, then somebody killed your horse and left you to die, and your

194

run-in with Townsend, and the little fracas I had with Starkey and Brown."

"Wait a minute," Nora said. "Gid, did you say you had a run-in with Del Starkey and Rhiny Brown?"

"Yes. Why, do you know them?" Gid asked.

"Oh yes, I know them," Nora answered. She shivered. "I know one of them too well," she added.

"They are also court deputies," John added. "They both work for Judge Huff."

"Actually, only one of them works for Huff," Gid said.

"No, both of them do," Nora insisted.

Gid shook his head. "Now, only Brown does. I killed Del Starkey," he said, matter-of-factly. "You going to eat that biscuit?"

Chapter Twenty-One

It had been less than an hour after Gid's bold rescue of his brother when John Woodward learned about the stay of execution. At first, John, angry by what happened, was going to confront Huff with the information. But Nora had a cooler head, reminding him that if Huff knew about it and didn't stop the hanging, then he might be dangerous to them as well.

John agreed, and without disclosing their intentions to anyone, he and Nora took the next coach out of Watson. They weren't sure Will and Gid would be in Gold Hill, but they did know that was where Will was headed when his horse was shot. And that information they kept to themselves.

At ten o'clock the previous night, after a long, grinding ride over rough roads, the coach stopped at a way-station. There, they were given a meal of ham, turnip greens, and cornbread. Afterward, John, Nora, and the other passengers slept fitfully on wooden benches in the waiting room. The hostler provided blankets for free, but the pillows rented for ten cents.

Two hours before dawn that morning, the coach got under way again, arriving in Gold Hill a little after eight. As a result of their long, hard trip, both John and Nora were very tired so, after breakfast, they took rooms in the hotel.

As the four of them checked in, Will paid particular attention to the room assignments. Nora was in room 211.

"We'll see you later today, after we've had a little rest," John said as he and his daughter started toward the stairs. "In the meantime, you boys stay out of trouble."

"Well, if we do get into trouble, I know a couple of pretty good lawyers," Will said.

John looked genuinely pleased by Will's response. "Thanks," he said.

"No, Mr. Woodward. I thank you."

Leaving the hotel, the two brothers walked along the sidewalk to the Land Office, their boots clumping loudly on the wide-plank boards. As they passed the notions shop, a woman stepped out in front of them. Gid recognized her immediately.

"Hello, Molly," Gid said, touching the brim of his hat.

"Gid, you've come back!" Molly said, squealing in

delight.

"I couldn't stay away," Gid teased.

"You broke my heart, you know," Molly said, extending her lower lip in a faux pout.

"Did I?"

"You did indeed."

Will laughed. "You'll have to excuse Gid, Miss. That's just the way he is. Why, if you just knew how he was, you wouldn't have anything to do with him. He's left a string of broken hearts all over the West."

"I'm sure he has," Molly replied. Then, noticing Will, she smiled, seductively. "And you have too, I'd be willing bet," she added flirtatiously. "Where are your manners, Gid? Aren't you going to introduce me to this, very handsome gentleman?"

"This is my brother, Will."

"Your brother? Oh, my, I can certainly see that attractive men run in the family. I do hope the two of you are going to come see me while you are here."

"I'll come see you, all right," Gid said. He nodded toward Will. "But as far as I'm concerned, Will can get his own girl."

"I don't think he'll have any trouble doing just that." Molly turned her attention back to Gid. "I'm counting on you coming to see me, just real soon." She looked at Will. "With, or without your brother."

With a toss of her curls, Molly hurried on down the board walk.

"I see you made a friend while you were here," Will said as they continued their walk.

"Well, you know me, Will. I'm a real friendly person."

"Uh, huh," Will replied laconically. He pointed to a building just in front of them. "There it is. Grant County Land Office."

The land office was a small, two-room lean-to shack that protruded from the side of the bank. Just inside the door was a counter that ran three-quarters of the way across the room. The north and east walls had windows, through which spilled a bright splash of sunlight. The west wall, which was actually the east wall of the bank building itself, was plastered with maps of Grant County. The back wall was lined with shelves. A door on the back wall led into another room.

Will stepped over to study the maps. Grant County was so large that it required four map sections to cover it.

"Where is this claim of yours?" Will asked.

"Right here," Gid said, pointing to one of the maps. "In the Mimbres Mountains."

"Hard to get there?"

"It's not a leisurely ride, but if we leave early in the morning, we should get there before nightfall," Gid said.

Will looked around the still empty room. "Wonder

where everyone is? It doesn't look as if anyone is that interested in doing business with us," he suggested.

"Maybe they didn't hear us. Hello? Anyone here?" Gid called.

There was a scurrying sound from the back room, then someone came through the door. "Sorry, gentlemen, I was busy and didn't hear you come in," the land-clerk apologized. He saw that they were looking at the maps. "Studying Grant County, are you? If you are looking to homestead, we have some choice sections available down in the valley. That's right about here," he said, crossing over to the map and pointing to the southern part of the county.

"We aren't looking to homestead," Gid said.

"Oh?" the clerk replied. "Then you are buying property somewhere? Excellent idea, sir. Some of the earlier property has been improved quite nicely."

"Not looking to buy, either," Gid said. "I've come to pick up the papers to my mining claim."

"Mining claim? Oh, yes," the clerk said. "I'm sorry, I guess I still haven't gotten used to the fact that those records are being kept here, now. They were moved down right after poor Mr. Bell was shot." He took a large notebook down from a shelf, blew the dust from it, then opened it. Removing his glasses, he began to polish them with his handkerchief. He looked up at Gid. "Do you have your claim number?"

"Yes," Gid said. "The claim number is two-five-one-four."

The clerk put his glasses back on. "Two-five-one-four," he repeated as he opened the notebook. Licking his fingers he turned several pages until he got to the page he was looking for. He ran his finger down the long column of numbers. "Ah, here it is. Two-five-one-four. Located up in the Mimbre Range, I believe?"

"That's it," Gid said. He smiled excitedly at Will.

The clerk moved his finger over to the right side of the page. "According to this, the claim papers haven't returned from the county seat at Silver City."

Gid's face reflected his frustration and disappointment. "Not back yet? Why not? How long does it take to post the claim?"

"I know that property deeds normally return within a week," the clerk said. "But I really don't have any experience in dealing with mineral claims. If you are concerned, though, you could send a telegram to the claims office in Silver City and make an inquiry."

"Yes," Gid said. "Yes, we might just do that. Thank you."

"Not at all," the land clerk replied. "Oh, and if your mine doesn't work out and you decide to go into farming, come back and see me. There are still some choice pieces of land remaining for anyone who will apply himself."

"Yeah, thanks again," Gid said.

Leaving the land office, Will and Gid went directly to the Western Union office.

"Good morning, Mr. Crain," Gid said.

"Good morning," Crain replied. He stared at Gid. "I know you, don't I? Didn't I send a telegram for you a few days ago?"

"No," Gid said. "You sold me a nostrum for a toothache."

Crain laughed. "A nostrum for a toothache," he said. "Very good. Yes, very good indeed."

Will looked at Gid with a quizzical expression on his face.

"It's an inside joke," Gid explained, reaching for one of the message pads. He carefully wrote his message and then handed it to Crain.

"How long you think it'll be before I hear back from them?" he asked.

"From the clerk of claims and deeds?" Crain replied. He looked up at the clock on the wall. "Knowing how they work, it'll take 'em a while before they get around to even reading your message. Then they'll have to go through the records. I doubt you'll hear anything back from them before mid to late afternoon."

"Then we'll see you this afternoon," Gid said.

"You take care of that toothache now," Crain called out, laughing at the joke.

Once outside, Gid rubbed his hands together and smiled. "Well, nothing to do now but wait," he said. "So what do you say we pay a call on Molly and some of her friends?"

"And, just what kind of call would that be, Little Brother? Social, or business?" Will asked.

"Will, with ladies like Molly and her friends, social calls are business calls."

Will chuckled. "That's what I thought."

"I like it like that. There's no misunderstanding, no beating around the bush. You know what you want, and they know what you want. So, what do you say? Shall we make that visit?"

"You go ahead," Will said. "I think I'll just wander around on my own for a while."

"Have it your own way," Gid said easily. "But as for me, when I've got a couple of hours to kill, and a room waiting, it's nice to have a willing woman to keep you company."

Will didn't disagree with his brother. The only place they parted company was on the choice of a willing woman. Will had his own choice in mind. What he didn't know was whether or not his choice would be willing.

Returning to the hotel, Will climbed the stairs up to the long, carpeted hallway of the second floor. Although three kerosene lanterns burned in the hallway, their chimneys were so blackened with smoke that the light was very dim, thus causing the hallway to be quite dark.

The doors to each room had been red at one time, though the paint was so distressed and flecked that it was difficult to tell the color. The door numbers, in faded white, were difficult, but not impossible to read.

Will stopped just outside 211 and knocked, lightly.

"Just a minute," a voice answered.

The door was pushed open just a crack, and Will saw Nora peering through. When she saw that it was Will, she exhibited a brief moment of surprise, which gave way to a broad smile. Stepping away from the door, she opened it to let him in. As soon as Will was inside, Nora stuck her head out into the hall and looked both ways. Satisfied that no one had seen him enter, she closed the door.

"I was hoping you would come," she said.

Chapter Twenty-Two

Molly met Gid in the downstairs drawing room of the sporting house where she worked, then led her upstairs to her room. From his position behind her, Gid could watch her butt wriggle inside the snug fit of the dress she was wearing.

"My room is down the hall...," Molly said.

"On the left," Gid interrupted. "I remember."

"You do? I'm flattered," Molly said. "I'm sure you've been in your share of such rooms."

Molly unlocked the door, then pushed it open, inviting Gid to go in first. The room, just as Gid remembered, was considerably larger than a normal hotel room. It was dominated by a four-poster bed, covered with a bright comforter. There were curtains to match, hanging at the windows.

The windows on the back wall looked out onto a

freight company, it's yards busy with departing and arriving wagons.

"You just going to stand there all day?" Molly asked. "Or is there something I could do that might get you interested in me?"

When Gid turned back around, he saw her working on the buttons at the back of her gown, watching him with smoky eyes and a provocative smile.

"Oh, I think you could get me interested," Gid replied.

A little over an hour later, Will, Gid, Nora, and John were having lunch together at Little Man's. Nora was bubbly and almost openly flirtatious with Will. A couple of times Will caught John looking at him, the expression in John's eyes indicating that he suspected something may have happened between Will and Nora. That same expression, however, said that John, who was just beginning to put his own life back together, wasn't about to criticize his daughter for anything she might have done.

After lunch the four of them walked over to the telegraph office to see if there was any reply to Gid's telegram.

"I've got it right here," Felix Crain said, handing Gid the message sheet. "I've got a feeling this isn't what you expected, though."

"What do you mean?" Gid asked, looking at Crain suspiciously.

"Maybe you'd better read it," Crain suggested.

Gid read it to himself. "What the hell?" he said.

"Read it aloud, Gid," Will said.

"This will confirm that all mineral rights, surface and subterranean, now relating to claim 2514 in the Mimbres Mountain Range henceforth and for a period of forty years, appertains to Judge Mason Huff," Gid read.

"What?" Will asked.

Gid looked up from the telegram. "How the hell did that son of a bitch get my claim?"

"I don't know," John replied. "But the fact that he has, explains a few things. Will, Judge Huff wasn't trying you. He was using the law to steal your brother's claim and to murder you."

"And he damn near did it," Will said.

"Yes, but what I want to know is...how the hell did he know I had filed a claim in the first place?" Gid asked.

"Yes, and how did he know about me? He not only knew I was your brother, he knew exactly where to find me."

"I might be able to answer that," Crain said.

Gid looked at the telegrapher. "What do you mean?"

Crain cleared his throat. "I, uh, am supposed to be sworn to secrecy," he said. "I'm not supposed to ever reveal anything that I send or receive. But Mr. Brown does represent the law so I, uh, thought it would be all right."

"What are you talking about?" John asked.

"Marshal Rhiny Brown asked me about you," Crain said to Gid. "He knew you had sent a telegram to someone, and he wanted to know who you sent it to."

"You told him, I suppose?"

"What was I to do?" Crain asked. "As I said, he is an officer of the court. I figured I didn't have any choice in the matter."

"Yes, but how did he even know to ask?" Gid asked. "I didn't say anything in the telegram about the claim."

"Maybe you didn't, but Milton Bell did," Crain said. "He was all excited about it, and he sent a wire to the county clerk of claims and deeds, telling about the ore that was brought in."

"When did he do that?"

Crain started looking through his records. "Here it is," he said. "He sent his telegram on the same day you sent yours. There was less than an hour between them."

"You said Brown asked about Mr. Crockett," John said. "By any chance, did Brown send a telegram?"

"Yes, I believe he did send one," Crain said. "It was in answer to a message he received from Judge Huff."

"He got one from Huff? What did that one say?" Will asked.

Crain shook his head. "I'm sorry, that was official county business. I can't tell you that."

"Mr. Crain, you know those toothache nostrums they

sell next door?" Gid asked.

"Yes?" Crain replied, guardedly.

"If you don't help us out here, there won't be enough nostrums in the entire apothecary to take care of you."

Intimidated by Gid's inference, Crain, with shaking hands, began rifling through his filed messages until he came up with one. "This is the one that came from Judge Huff," he said.

GOLD FOUND NEAR GOLD HILL. CLAIM FILED BY GID CROCKETT

Will read the message, then passed it around to the others.

"What did Brown say in answer?" Gid asked.

Crain handed yet another message over to Gid.

INFORMATION HERE IS THAT GID CROCKETT HAS BROTHER IN THORNBURG NAMED WILL. WILL TAKE CARE OF THE SITUATION.

"I can't believe they would actually put in the telegram that they are going to try and kill us," Gid said.

John chuckled, and shook his head. "My boy, you should look at things with a lawyer's eyes," he suggested. "Whereas we don't have the slightest doubt as to what they are talking about, there is not one intimidating word in either of those telegrams."

Ten minutes later, the four were discussing all their options at a table in a saloon called the Gold Hill Watering Hole.

"Here you are. Three beers and one..." the waiter paused, then let the word slide out derisively, "Sarsaparilla. You are a little old for this kind of drink, aren't you Mister?"

The four had just ordered drinks, and it was John's request for a sarsaparilla that brought on the waiter's sarcasm.

"Waiter," Gid said easily. "Is there a good doctor in this town?"

"Yes, there's ole' Doc Fontaine. He has an office over the general store. Why?" He glanced toward John. "Are you afraid the sarsaparilla is too strong for your friend?" The waiter laughed at his own joke.

"No," Gid said. "I was just wondering who we could summon to pull my boot out of your ass."

The waiter looked at Gid as if about to respond then, noticing Gid's size, made a quick reassessment of his options. He chose the wiser course.

"I'll, uh...be over there if you need any more drinks," he said, beating a hasty retreat.

John laughed. "Watching the expression on that man's face was almost worth having to drink this," he said, holding the soft drink in front of him and studying it without enthusiasm. "If I am honest with myself, I'll never again drink anything any stronger than this."

Nora put her hand on her father's arm. "I'm very proud of you, Pa," she said.

John put his hand on his daughter's. "That, alone, is enough to make me drink this stuff." He took a swallow. "It's not all that bad," he said as he screwed his face up in distaste.

The others laughed.

"Gid, when you found the ore, did you make a quick claim?" John asked.

"Yes, I did."

"Were there any witnesses?"

"No. I just wrote it out on a piece of paper, signed it, put it in a tin can and buried it."

"Too bad there weren't any witnesses," John said. "If there are witnesses to a quick claim, and that quick claim pre-dates a filing with the office of claims and deeds, the quick claim will be accepted as the more valid of the two documents."

"Why don't we witness it?" Nora asked.

John shook his head. "We can't," he answered. "As I said, the date of witnessing must precede the date of filing."

"Who would know?" Nora asked.

"I would know," John replied. "And as an officer of the court, for me to do such a thing would be the same thing as committing perjury."

"You would let something like that stand in your way, even though you know that Huff and Brown are stealing the claim from Gid?" Nora asked.

John shook his head, then looked across the table at Will and Gid. "I'm sorry, Will, Gid," he said. "I hope you understand."

"Don't worry about it," Will said easily. "I'm pretty sure we'll find Huff and Brown out at Gid's claim. And if they are there, we'll just have a face-to-face meeting with them. I'm sure we will be able negotiate a solution to our problems."

"Would you let me go with you?" Nora asked.

"Nora, don't talk nonsense," John said. "Huff and Brown are dangerous men."

"Rhiny Brown was one of the men who raped me," Nora said. "And I know now that Huff not only knew it, he countenanced it. He denied us justice the last time, but I will have my day in court."

"Then I'm going too," John said.

"Pa, there's no need for you to put yourself in danger."

"You don't really think I would let you go by yourself, do you?"

"I won't be by myself. Will and Gid will be with

me. That is...if you will let me go," she added, looking directly at Will.

"I never try and talk another person out of doin' what has to be done," Will said. "If you want to come with us, come ahead. That goes for both of you," he added."

"Then, I'm coming as well," John insisted.

Chapter Twenty-Three

Gid led Will, Nora, and John into the Mimbres Mountain Range to the general area where he had made his gold find and staked his quick claim. It was dark by the time they got there and, ahead of them, they could see the faint glow of a campfire. Gid pointed out that the campfire was almost exactly where his claim was.

"You think its Huff and Brown?" Nora asked.

"Could be. Why don't you two wait here while Gid and I take a look?" Will said. His suggestion, which was more in the form of an order, wasn't questioned.

Pistols in hand, Will and Gid started toward the glow of the campfire. Within seconds they were swallowed up by the darkness so that Nora and John, even though they knew Will and Gid were nearby, suddenly felt as if they were all alone.

An owl hooted.

A distant coyote called.

The wind whistled.

Nora shivered.

"Are you cold or afraid?" John asked.

"A little of both," Nora admitted.

"Yes," John replied. He put his arm around his daughter. "Me too."

A quarter of a mile away, Will and Gid were moving quickly through the night. By now they were close enough to the glowing campfire to overhear voices and Will reached out to touch his brother in a signal to stop.

"That's Huff's voice," he whispered.

"I can't believe you could be so damn dumb that you didn't even check this out," they heard Huff saying in a loud, angry voice.

"You didn't say anything about checking out the claim site," another voice answered. "All you said was to take care of the Crockett brothers." igloo

"Yes, well, you couldn't even do that, could you?" Huff said.

"The Crocketts ain't ordinary men."

"I only heard Brown's voice one time," Gid whispered. "But that sounds like him."

"Are you saying there's no gold here at all?" a third voice asked. Neither Will nor Gid were able to recognize the voice.

"That's what I'm saying," Huff replied. "We've done all this for nothing."

"But, what about the ore Crockett brought in?" Brown asked. "Before I killed Bell, he told me he was holdin' at least a thousand dollars' worth. Where did that come from?"

"Yeah, that had to come from somewhere," still a fourth voice said. "It didn't just drop out of the sky."

"As a matter fact, it did fall from the sky," Huff said.

"What do you mean if fell from the sky?" Brown asked.

"Five years ago the Lucifer mine had about a week's worth of ore, all dug up waiting to be hauled out. They also had a lot of powder on hand, to use to open up another shaft. Somehow the powder exploded and it caused a rock slide, including the ore. From time to time, some of that ore is still being found. Crockett just happened to stumble across a little pocket of it, that's all. He thought he'd hit the mother lode. In fact, all he found was a scrap pile."

"Did he get all of it?" By now, Will and Gid were close enough to see the four men sitting around the campfire. "Maybe there's some left."

"Starkey had more gold in that tooth of his than there is here," Huff replied.

"No gold? Damn," Gid said quietly. "And all this time,

I thought we were rich."

"Which one is Brown?" Will asked.

"He's the short, hairy son of a bitch," Gid said. "Oh, and I've run across those other two bastards, too. They are the ones who jumped me in Thornburg."

Suddenly a fifth voice called out. The voice came from the dark, from the left, or south side of the campfire, Will and Gid having approached the fire from the east.

"Judge! Don't shoot! I'm comin' in, and I've got some people with me!"

"Who the hell is that?" Gid asked.

"Sounds like Lewis's voice," Will replied.

"Come on in, Lewis," Huff called back, confirming Will's suspicion.

Will and Gid watched as three figures moved into the golden bubble of light.

"Oh hell!" Will said.

Walking in front of Lewis, with their hands raised, were John and Nora Woodward.

"Only one of us should've come," Gid said. "The other one of us should have stayed with them."

"Too late to worry about that now," Will replied.

"Well, well, if it isn't two thirds of Watson's legal community," Huff said in a sarcastic welcome. "Where did you find them?"

"I found them about a quarter of a mile back," Lewis

ROBERT VAUGHAN

said.

"What are you doing up here?" Huff asked.

"As you know, I haven't had that much success as a lawyer lately," John said. "So we came up here to prospect for gold."

Huff laughed, a sharp, brittle laugh. "I have to hand it to you, Mr. Woodward, you do have a droll sense of humor." The smile left his face. "I'll ask you again. What are you doing here?"

"There's two more out there somewhere," Lewis said. "I found four horses."

"Four horses, you say? Interesting. Who is with you?" he asked. "Where are the others?"

"Nobody came with us," John answered. "The other two horses are packhorses, in case we found gold.

"Packhorses with saddles?" Lewis scoffed. "Who are you kidding?"

"I must give you credit, Mr. Woodward. You are displaying more courage than one might expect from a drunken fool."

"My father is no longer a drunk," Nora said resolutely.

"Perhaps not. But he is still a fool. All four of you are, thinking you could get the better of me. Now, who is with you?"

"Whoever it is, I'll get them in," Brown said. He drew his pistol and pointed it at Nora's head. Nora closed

218

her eyes tightly.

"Brown! No!" John shouted. "If you must shoot someone, shoot me!"

"Oh, I will," Brown replied. "I'm going to shoot both of you if your two friends don't come in with their hands up...right now."

"Judge Huff! You can't let this happen!" John pleaded.

Huff shrugged his shoulders. "I'm like Pontius Pilate," he said. "I wash my hands of this. I'm sure you know that Mr. Brown is a man with a violent nature. If he says he is going to shoot your daughter unless your friends show themselves, then I have no doubt that he will."

"If anyone is out there," Brown said. "This is your last chance."

After Brown's call there was a beat of silence, broken by the sound of the cylinder being engaged as he pulled the hammer back.

"No, please!" John shouted.

"Hold it!" Will called from outside the bubble of light. "Don't shoot her. We're coming in!"

With their hands raised, Will and Gid emerged from the darkness.

"It's good to see you again, Mr. Crockett," Huff said to Will. Brown was still holding the pistol to Nora's head. "Or, should I say the misters Crockett, since you are obviously Gid Crockett."

Gid said nothing.

"You may lower the pistol, Mr. Brown."

Brown lowered his gun.

"You are the son of a bitch that nearly blinded me," one of the men said bitterly, looking at Gid. His face, as well as the face of the man standing next to him, was discolored with bruises.

"I'm sure you recognize these two gentlemen," Huff said, nodding toward the two men. "When I learned you had gone to Thornburg, I sent Mr. Garriga and Mr. Chandler to kill you. They failed, and I must say, they came out somewhat the worse for their encounter with you."

"That's what happens when you send boys to do a man's job," Gid said.

"Dixon, Washburn, Starkey, Townsend... they're dead too, because of the two of you,"

"Judge, what do you want to do with them?" Lewis asked.

"I know what I aim to do with this one," Brown said. He looked at Nora with eyes that were deep and evil. Reflecting the flickering light of the flames, it was like looking into hell itself. Shivering, Nora moved toward her father. John put his arm around her.

"No need goin' to your daddy, little girl," Brown said. "He can't help you." Brown rubbed himself. "It was good last time...but it's goin' to be even better this time."

"Don't you touch her," John said.

Brown laughed. "You couldn't do anything about it last time, what makes you think you can this time?"

"That's enough of that," Huff said. "Mr. Lewis, you raised a good question. What are we going to do with them?" He looked toward Will. "Of course, Mr. Will Crockett's fate has already been decided. I sentenced him to hang, and he is going to do just that." He looked at Gid. "And so will this one, for interfering in the discharge of a court-ordered execution."

"You can't hang them," John said. "The governor granted a stay, pending a new trial. And everyone in Watson knows that by now."

"An astute observation, Mr. Woodward, but I have no intention of returning to Watson," Huff said. "As a circuit judge, I have the authority to incorporate a community anywhere three or more people request incorporation. Gentlemen...and lady," he said, with a deferential nod toward Nora. "I hereby incorporate this site as the town of Goldslide. And, until such time as an election can be conducted, I appoint you, Mr. Garriga, as the mayor, and you, Mr. Chandler, as the town marshal. Gentlemen, disarm the prisoners and carry out the sentence."

Grinning, the newly appointed "marshal" and "mayor" started toward Will and Gid with guns drawn. John, who had moved slowly, and unobserved, toward the fire, suddenly kicked up a burning brand. Glowing cinders went into Lewis's eyes, and with a shout of pain, he dropped his pistol.

"Now!" Will shouted.

With Garriga and Chandler momentarily distracted by John's action, Will and Gid were able to draw and fire. The night was lit by gun flashes. Garriga and Chandler, both of whom already had their weapons drawn, fired, but their missiles flew harmlessly into the dark, whereas both Will and Gid's bullets found their mark.

"No! No! Don't shoot! Don't shoot!" Huff shouted in fear, throwing his hands in the air. Brown, not willing to go against the Crocketts alone, followed suit. Lewis had no choice but to follow because John had picked up Lewis's dropped pistol. The positions were now reversed. Those who had, but a heartbeat earlier, been the captors, were now prisoners.

Chapter Twenty-Four

The sun was full, firing the mountains with color and pushing back the chill. Will was sitting near the fire, drinking coffee. Gid was chewing on a piece of jerky. Looking sullen and a little frightened by the change in their fortunes, Huff, Brown, and Lewis were sitting by the fire. John was poking at the fire with a stick.

Nora was still asleep.

"I gotta piss," Brown said.

"So, piss."

"How'm I goin' to do that? My hands is tied."

Will started over toward him to untie his hands. As he did so, he saw something in Brown's pocket. "What's this?" he asked, reaching for it.

"That's mine," Brown said.

Will pulled it out. "I know this watch," he said.

He remembered now. This was the watch Lurleen had

worn on the dress she called her schoolmarm dress. "This belonged to Lurleen Simpson. Gid told me she had been murdered, but I didn't think it had any connection to this. You killed her, didn't you?"

"What if I did?" Brown replied. "It's not like anyone is going to cry over her. Hell, she wasn't nothin' but a whore. Killin' her was as easy as steppin' on a bug."

Will felt the anger boiling up inside. He drew back his hand to hit him, then turned and walked away to keep from hitting a man who couldn't hit back.

"Where you goin'? I told you I have to piss," Brown said again.

"Piss in your pants, you son of a bitch," Will growled.

"What do you plan to do with us?" Huff asked.

"I don't know. Turn you over to the law, I suppose."

Huff laughed. "What law? I'm a judge; Brown and Lewis are law officers. Do you really think anyone would take your word against mine? Especially when I tell them you killed Mayor Garriga and Marshall Chandler as they were discharging their duty as officials of Goldslide."

"There is no town of Goldslide," Will said.

"Oh, but there is. As a circuit judge, I have the authority to issue a court order declaring the incorporation of a town and I have incorporated Goldslide."

Will looked at John. "Is that right?"

"As ludicrous as it may seem, circuit judges do have the

right to do that," John said. He held his arm out. "Welcome to Goldslide, population, seven."

"There is a way out," Huff suggested. "Let us go, and I'll reverse my decision. I'll declare you innocent in the Townsend case. I'll also rule that you killed Garriga and Chandler in self-defense." Huff looked at John. "I'll even reverse my decision on the rape case. I'll declare Townsend and Brown guilty."

"Hold it!" Brown said. "You're turnin' on your own friends?"

"Brown, disabuse yourself of any idea that you and I were ever friends," Huff said. "You are a pig of a man. You have been useful to me, but you have never been and could never be a friend."

"You know, Huff, I should've killed you a long time ago," Brown sneered.

"What about my offer?" Huff said to Will.

"We're supposed to do this and just all go on our way?" Will asked.

"Sure, why not?" Huff replied. "It turns out there's no gold here anyway. We have no reason to fight."

"Are we also to just forget about the innocent people who were murdered?" John asked. "The assayer and the girl in Thornburg?"

"I didn't kill them. Brown did," Huff said. "Besides, that has nothing to do with what is going on here."

Will stood up and walked away from the others. He looked out across the valley. The closest mountains were gold and silver in the morning sun. Each range beyond the first range progressed in color, from bright blue to deep purple. If such a place as Goldslide really did exist, its residents would have a beautiful view.

Suddenly Will smiled then turned and walked back to the fire. "We're going to have an election," he said.

"What?" John asked.

"Mayor Garriga and Marshall Chandler are dead. The town of Goldslide needs new officers. John, I nominate you as mayor, my brother as marshal, and myself as judge."

"What are you doing?" Huff asked. There was a frightened edge to his voice as he began to consider the possibilities.

"Are there any further nominations?"

Gid and John stared at Will as if he had suddenly gone mad.

"No? Then all nominations are closed. Those who are in favor of the slate of candidates as presented, signify by raising your right hand." Will raised his hand, followed by Gid, and then, rather reluctantly, by John. By now they realized that Will had something in mind, but they didn't know what.

"The slate of candidates has been duly elected." He turned to Huff. "Now, I can turn you in to the law," he said. "In fact, I'm turning you over to myself, because you, Brown, and Lewis are going to be tried for murder in the court of Goldslide."

"What? Don't be ridiculous! You can't do that!" Huff said.

"Oh, but I can...and I will," Will said. "And, thanks to your court order...it will be legal."

"Wait a minute, Will, are you serious?" John asked.

Will looked at the three prisoners. "I'm dead serious," he said. "We are going to try these three men right now, right here, in this newly incorporated town of Goldslide. And after we find them guilty, we are going to hang them from that tree right over there."

Huff, Brown, and Lewis blanched. In the morning light, their faces looked gray as mud-clay at a spring.

"You can't do this," Brown said. "You got no right to do this."

"Oh, but I do. Judge Huff provided the authority for me to do it. In fact, he was going to hold court himself, I believe."

"What about counsel?" Huff asked. "You can't have court without counsel."

"By a fortuitous set of circumstances, we have two lawyers here," Will said. By now Nora was awake, and, quietly, John was filling her in on what was going on. "I intend to appoint one of them as your defense counsel and the other as prosecutor. You have your choice as to who you want."

"Some choice we have," Huff said, scoffing. He nodded toward the two Woodwards. "Either a drunk or a female who hasn't yet passed the bar."

"That may be, but it is the only choice you have," Will said.

The three prisoners huddled together for a moment, then Huff spoke for them. "If there is no way out of this... then we choose John Woodward to defend us."

"So ordered," Will said.

John and Nora came over to speak to Will.

"You didn't ask us how we feel about this," John said.

"How do you feel about it?"

"We don't want to do it."

"All right," Will said easily.

"That's it? You've changed your mind? You aren't going to have the trial?"

"Huff's right. We can't have a trial without lawyers, and you don't want to do it. So, I may as well shoot them," Will said. He started toward the prisoners, pulling his pistol as he did so.

"Wait!" John called out to him.

Will paused and looked back at him.

"What are you going to do?"

"I told you, I'm going to shoot them," Will said easily.

"Just like that?"

"Just like that."

"How can you do such a thing?"

"Were you in the war, John?"

"Uh, no," John replied.

"I didn't think so. Let me tell you, John, there were a lot of men killed during the war. In fact, I killed a lot of men during the war. Many of the men I killed...I would say that most of the men I killed...were good men. Family men, many of them, with a wife and kids at home. They were in the war fighting for what they believed in... just as I was. Now, I don't feel good about having killed those good men, John, but it was war, and good men were killing good men on both sides."

Will pointed at the three prisoners. "Now, as far as I'm concerned, these men aren't good men. They are pond scum. Now, after all the good men I've killed, do you think I would have a moment's hesitation in shooting men like these?"

Will raised his pistol and pointed it at Huff, then came back on the hammer.

"Wait!" John called. "We'll do it! We'll hold the trial."

An eagle soared overhead with a struggling mouse in its talons. Below that majestic bird's flight path, a strange scene was taking place on the side of a mountain.

Six men and one woman, isolated from their fellow creatures by many miles, dotted the landscape below in a precise manner. Will was sitting authoritatively upon a log. Nora stood just to one side of the log, while Gid sat on a rock a few feet away. Huff, Brown, and Lewis stood with their hands tied behind them. John conferred earnestly with them.

"I now call this court to order," Will said. He nodded toward Gid. "Gid will act as a juror. I will be both judge and juror. We are convened to try Mason Huff, Rhiny Brown, and Emil Lewis on the charges of murder, conspiracy to murder, rape, misappropriation of a mining claim, and robbery. How do you plead?"

"Your honor, defense moves that the charge of rape be dropped from the indictment," John said.

"Are you arguing that Brown did not rape your daughter?" Will asked, surprised by John's petition.

"I am not arguing that," John said. "Whether he did, or did not rape Miss Woodward is irrelevant."

"How can it be irrelevant?"

"He has already been tried for that charge and found not guilty. The principle of double jeopardy prohibits him from being tried for the same charge a second time."

"All right, the charge of rape is dropped," Will said. "How do the defendants plead to the remaining charges?"

"They have refused to plea, Your Honor, so I will enter

a plea for them. I plead not guilty."

"Mr. Woodward, you know damned well they are guilty," Will said in exasperation. "How can you plead them not guilty?"

"If they remain mute I have no choice but to plead not guilty on their behalf," John replied. "If this court is to have any validity at all, then we must follow the law."

Will stroked his chin for a moment, then he nodded. "All right," he said. "Court accepts a plea of not guilty. Prosecution, you may begin."

"Your Honor," John said again.

Will sighed. "What now, Mr. Woodward?"

"Your Honor, not only have the defendants refused to plead, but they have also refused to testify."

"No problem. I'll just order them to testify."

"You can't do that. No one can be forced to testify against themselves."

"Whose side are you on?" Will asked in exasperation.

"I'm an advocate for the defense, but I am on the side of the law," John said. "What I'm saying is, since the defendants refuse to testify in their own behalf, we have no witnesses. With no witnesses, I see no need for opening statements. If there is no objection from the prosecution, I recommend that we go directly to summation."

"Do you object to that, Miss Woodward?" Will asked Nora.

"I have no objections, Your Honor."

"Very well, the court will hear summation. Mr. Woodward, you may begin. But, before you begin, let me tell you that you cannot make the argument that this court has no jurisdiction. You will make your summation exactly as if you were trying this case in any city in the country."

"Your Honor, under ordinary circumstances, I would petition the court to sever the case so that each defendant could stand trial on his own. Since these aren't ordinary circumstances, I will plead as if the cases are severed.

"I begin with the case against Emil Lewis. I have personally known Lewis for at least five years. I know him to be a man of less than average intelligence, who is mean-spirited and foul-mouthed. Such a person can be easily led by someone in authority, such as Mason Huff. Lewis wears a badge, and Huff is a circuit judge. Therefore, Lewis's very presence here is the result of his genuine belief that he is acting in the line of the duty of his office.

"Low intelligence, mean spirit, a foul mouth, and acquiescence to authority are not, of themselves, violations of the law. I have never witnessed Lewis commit murder, conspire to commit murder, nor indeed, break the law in any way. And I am certain this court will be unable to produce a witness who will testify otherwise. I therefore suggest that Emil Lewis be found totally innocent of all charges.

"With regard to Rhiny Brown, I plead not guilty."

"How can you plead him not guilty?" Will demanded. He pointed to Brown. "He confessed to killing Lurleen Simpson."

"Your Honor, please. Allow me to conduct my case," John said.

"Yeah, all right. Go ahead," Will said.

"Brown is not guilty by reason of insanity. You are correct, Your Honor, when you say that, with our own ears, we heard Brown admit to murdering Lurleen Simpson. We also heard him say that killing her was no more traumatic for him than stepping on a bug.

"I submit to you that no one can kill as easily as stepping on a bug, unless it is the result of an aberrant mental condition. Another word for aberrant mental behavior is insane. And, in our legal system, someone who is insane—even criminally insane—cannot be held accountable for their actions. Rhiny Brown is obviously insane and, therefore, not guilty.

"And, finally, we come to Judge Mason Huff. Judge Huff is, admittedly, the most difficult of the three to put a handle on. He is a brilliant and learned man who, for some time, has occupied a position of power and prestige. Such men sometimes step outside society's boundaries, simply because the temptation to do so is matched by the power to do so.

"There is no doubt that Judge Huff is such a man. However, we are convened to try him, not for malfeasance in office, but for murder and conspiracy to commit murder. And, whereas we have validation from Brown's own lips that he committed murder, we have no such confession from Judge Huff. I submit, therefore, that without compelling evidence, eyewitnesses who can testify to fact, or his confession, we have no choice but to find Mason Huff not guilty.

"Defense rests."

Chapter Twenty-Five

Although John Woodward was defending the man who had raped her, as well as the man who had given the rapist a pass in that mockery of a trial two years earlier, Nora Woodward was never more proud of her father than she was at this very moment. There, on the side of a mountain, in a raw and lawless land, she had seen law practiced by a man of principle and dignity.

"Is prosecution ready for summation?" Will asked.

"I am." Nora said.

"I hope you are," Will said. "Because the truth is, your father has put up a powerful defense for the indefensible."

Nora looked over at her father and at the three defendants. "He has, hasn't he?" she said, proudly.

"Make your case, girl," Will said, not as a judge, but as a man who truly wanted to see justice done.

"Your Honor, the defense made an effort to sever the

case in his presentation. It is his contention that Emil Lewis is not guilty by reason of low intelligence and lack of self-esteem...that Rhiny Brown is innocent by reason of insanity...and that Mason Huff is not guilty because of the lack of any factual witnesses or a confession.

"But I would argue that the case cannot be severed. We cannot plead their cases individually, because while we are dealing with more than one person, we are also dealing with the unifying charge of conspiracy. A conspiracy is a whole, and once something becomes whole, it can never again be separated. Apple pie consists of apples, sugar, flour, cinnamon, and butter. Those are all individual things but, once they are assembled and baked, they become a pie, and no matter how small a piece you cut...you always have apple pie.

"That being the case, Your Honor, the guilt of one of these defendants is the guilt of all of them. Therefore, as the prosecutor, I am going to focus on the one for whom we do have hard evidence, in the form of a watch that he stole from the body of his victim. We also have a confession.

"By his own words, Brown is guilty of murder. We don't know how many more murders he has committed, but we do know that he attempted to murder Will and Gid Crockett.

"Defense has suggested that Brown might be insane,

for no sane person, he says, could kill someone as easily as stepping on a bug. But I say we must disallow the plea of insanity in order to find this man, and these men, guilty as charged. But how can we find him sane? For what sane man could commit crimes with such lack of passion?

"The answer is...no man could, if we gauge sanity by the standards of moral men. But this man...these men...are not moral. Therefore the only test of sanity we need to hold up to the light is whether he was a man of reason when he committed the crime. Was Rhiny Brown a man of reason?

"I call your attention to the fact that he held a gun to my head. He then announced in a loud voice that he would shoot me...and my father. His reason for that was to force you, Your Honor, and you, Mr. Juror, to come in from the dark with your hands in the air. He was therefore aware that the threat to kill me was something that would disturb you. He could not reason such a thing unless he had the tool of reason in the grasp of his mind. He could not threaten if he was not aware that killing was an evil thing.

"Therefore, Your Honor, I submit that Rhiny Brown is fully in possession of reason and is aware of right from wrong. That awareness of right and wrong is all that is required for him to be legally sane.

"If you accept this logic, then you must declare him

sane, and if he is sane, then he stands convicted, and condemned by his own words.

"If justice is truly to be served in this court of ours, if the truth will out here on this lonely mountainside in the midst of some of the most beautiful country God ever created, then there can be only one verdict rendered, and that verdict is guilty. And, because they are part of a conspiracy—part of a whole—the guilt of Rhiny Brown is the guilt of them all.

"The prosecution rests."

"Court will recess while the jury decides," Will said. Nodding at his brother, he got up from the log and the two of them walked away for a little distance to discuss the verdict.

"What do you think?" Gid asked.

"The girl was good, wasn't she?" Will asked.

"Yes, she was. But so was the father," Gid replied.

"Yeah. Especially his argument about Lewis. I think he's right. I think Lewis is just an ignorant shit that got caught up in this. He was too damn dumb to get out of it."

"What about the girl saying you can't separate them?" Gid asked.

"She made a good point, I agree. But I figure this is a hanging case, and like John said, a fella ought not to be hung just because he's dumb. I say we find Huff and Brown guilty, and we cut Lewis loose."

"All right," Gid agreed.

Returning, Will called the court back to order.

"It is the decision of this court that the defendant, Emil Lewis, be found not guilty."

"What?" Lewis said, a broad smile on his face. "You're findin' me not guilty?"

"Untie him, Gid."

Gid untied Lewis and Lewis began immediately to rub his wrists.

"Step away from the other prisoners please," Will said.

"Yes, sir!" Lewis said. He started toward his gun, then stopped and looked up at Will. "Is it all right if I pick up my gun?"

"Yes," Will said. "But keep it in your holster."

"What about us?" Huff said.

"The court finds Mason Huff and Rhiny Brown guilty and sentences you both to hang. Sentence to be carried out immediately. Lewis, help my brother get these two mounted."

"Yes, sir," Lewis said, as subservient now to Will as he had been to Huff before.

"Your Honor, I object!" John Woodward shouted.

"On what grounds, counselor?"

"On the grounds that a summary execution, without giving defense time for an appeal, is little more than a lynching. And if we go through with this, then I remind you of the prosecutor's analogy of an apple pie. We will all be guilty of lynching, and lynching is murder. We will be no better than the men we have just found guilty."

"As prosecutor, I agree with counsel for defense," Nora said. "If we are truly a constituted court, then we must allow for a right of appeal."

"Court will stand in recess," Will said.

Will asked his brother to take a walk with him.

"What are you going to do, Will?" Gid asked.

"What do you think I should do, Little Brother?"

"If there was ever anybody who needed hangin', it's those two sons of bitches," Gid said.

"I agree with you, but if you will notice, even the prosecutor agreed with defense counsel that they should be given the right of appeal."

"That's just because she's his daughter," Gid said.

"No, it's because Nora and John are the only true representatives of the law, and I'm not inclined to go against them. I'm going to grant them time to appeal."

Thornburg, one month later:

Gid was in the Desert Strike Saloon with Suzy Jenkins. Gid was enjoying a beer while Suzy was drinking tea.

Will came in then with a smile on his face, carrying a folded newspaper.

"What do you have there, Will?"

"Vindication of my short career as a judge," Will said, laying the paper on the table. "This is the Albuquerque Sun Times."

SENTENCING OF RHINY BROWN AND MASON HUFF UPHELD

Arguing before the New Mexico Appeals Court, Attorney Nora Woodward made a brilliant case upholding the trial and sentencing of Rhiny Brown and Mason Huff in the newly constituted court of the town of Goldslide.

John Woodward argued for the defense before Appellate Judge Ambrose Wilson but despite his well-constructed presentation, the crimes of the two defendants were too heinous for any clemency to be granted.

Judge Wilson upheld the sentence given by Judge William Crockett and at dawn the following day, in the privacy of the prison yard, the two men were hanged.

"Damn, big brother, hope you don't expect me to call you judge." Gid said.

"I find you in contempt of court," Will teased. "And your fine is one glass of beer."

"Can I appeal?"

"What do you say, Suzy, can he appeal?"

"Appeal denied," Suzy said with a big smile.

A Look At: The Town That Wouldn't Die (The Crocketts' Western Saga: Four)

Bringing justice, no matter the cost in this western folklore!

Normally the Crockett brothers paid no mind to some varmint's love life. But Will and Gid were down to their last dollars, so they agreed to find the guy's long-lost lover, a little filly named Cat Clay. But Cat was living in the middle of a Mexican ranch war – with bullets flying thicker than blazes. Now, Will and Gid Crockett have to find a killer, settle a ranch dispute and rescue a lovely lady without going six feet under. All in a day's work...

AVAILABLE SEPTEMBER 2021

About the Author

Robert Vaughan sold his first book when he was 19. That was 57 years and nearly 500 books ago. He wrote the novelization for the mini-series Andersonville. Vaughan wrote, produced, and appeared in the History Channel documentary Vietnam Homecoming.

His books have hit the NYT bestseller list seven times. He has won the Spur Award, the PORGIE Award (Best Paperback Original), the Western Fictioneers Lifetime Achievement Award, received the Readwest President's Award for Excellence in Western Fiction, is a member of the American Writers Hall of Fame and is a Pulitzer Prize nominee.

Vaughan is also a retired army officer, helicopter pilot with three tours in Vietnam. And received the Distinguished Flying Cross, the Purple Heart, The Bronze Star with three oak leaf clusters, the Air Medal for valor with 35 oak leaf clusters, the Army Commendation Medal, the Meritorious Service Medal, and the Vietnamese Cross of Gallantry.

www.ingramcontent.com/pod-product-compliance
Lightning Source LLC
Chambersburg PA
CBHW011434240626
47153CB00011B/2985